CHRISTMAS ON PEACH TREE LANE

JULES BENNETT

carina
press

carina
press®

Recycling programs
for this product may
not exist in your area.

ISBN-13: 978-1-335-91833-8

Christmas on Peach Tree Lane

Carina Press
22 Adelaide St. West, 40th Floor
Toronto, Ontario M5H 4E3, Canada
www.CarinaPress.com

Printed in U.S.A.

Special thanks to Elaine for absolutely everything.

CHRISTMAS ON PEACH TREE LANE

Chapter One

Don't get your tinsel in a tangle.
* Violet Calhoun

"You get a headband, you get a headband. Everybody gets a headband."

Violet Calhoun tossed reindeer antler headbands to her best friends, Simone and Robin. Robin put her festive accessory in place between her bangs and ponytail while Simone twirled hers between her fingertips and glared.

"Why do we have to do this every year? It's not even Halloween, yet," Simone complained.

Robin laughed. "Dates are irrelevant with Violet and we do this because we love her…tacky headbands and all."

While they were all the very best of friends, and had been since they were forced into a group science project in first grade, Simone didn't embrace the holidays quite the same way Violet did. Violet figured Robin just appeased her to keep the peace.

Actually, Violet didn't know anyone who embraced this season in her enthusiastic way. Obviously that's why she'd been deemed the best candidate to spearhead the Tinsel Tour every December here in Peach Grove, Georgia.

Decorating historic Southern mansions in a million twinkle lights, garland, gold and red ribbons, and anything else she could find for that wow factor was seriously what she lived for. Each home had a theme and each one was magical in its own, charming way. Twelve months out of the year she was seeking inspiration and new décor.

"Don't you think it's a bit early to start wearing these?" Simone asked.

Violet adjusted hers and fluffed her long curls around her shoulders. "I'm going as a human Christmas stocking to the town carnival."

Robin shrugged. "I like it. Creative."

"Creative?" Simone laughed. "She's something Christmasy every year. Although the human snow globe was pretty cool. Creative would be if she went as a Playboy Bunny or even a typical witch."

Violet gasped. "You'll never see me in either of those costumes, thank you very much. And the event is for the community with families, not a tasteless bachelorette party."

"Well, I'm going as a Greek goddess," Robin declared. "It's comfortable and pretty, which are two components I want in my Halloween costume."

"What about you?" Violet asked Simone. "Wait. Let me guess. You're doing the Playboy Bunny?"

Simone pursed her lips. "Funny, but no. I opted for Jasmine from *Aladdin*."

Violet gasped. "Ooh, you'll look sexy. I like it."

"Thank you. I haven't been working out these past six months to hide this new body." Simone gave a mock bow. "So, where's Mama Lori?"

Violet's mother was always with them. Growing up,

the three girls were always together and usually at Violet's house where Lori was always treating each of them as her own. When they were teens, Robin's mother passed away suddenly and then after graduation, Simone's mother took off with her free-spirited boyfriend and they barely visited Peach Grove. So, the three adopted Lori as their group mother and often included her in their GNO.

"Mom isn't going to make it," she told her friends. "She's out with Porter again."

"Whoa," Robin exclaimed. "Weren't they just out last night?"

Violet nodded. "They've been seeing each other for about four months now. I'm really happy for her."

Her parents had divorced when Violet was fifteen, but they'd parted on good terms. They hadn't been in love for years and had just stayed together for her. When her father remarried, Violet and her mother went to the ceremony. Violet loved how her parents remained not only supportive of everything she did, but also friends with each other. Sometimes people could love each other and just not be meant for each other—her parents were proof of that.

And now her mother was giddy like a teenager with a new crush and Violet couldn't be happier. Lori Calhoun had dated over the years, but nobody had captured her attention like city mayor Porter Crosby.

"Good for her," Simone chimed in. "I'm glad someone has come into her life that pulls her away from us. She deserves to date and find love."

"I don't know that she's looking for long term," Violet said. "She's been independent for so long, but I agree. I'm glad she's found someone to go out with."

"I hope you didn't make her wear a damn headband," Simone mumbled.

"I mean, really, like I'd do that."

Violet wasn't about to mention that she had taken her mother a festive headband with a small light-up Christmas tree earlier in the day.

Sipping on her pinot, Violet glanced across to her two friends. "So, while I have you guys here—"

"Please don't say it," Simone demanded.

Violet merely smiled. They truly did have that special bond where she rarely had to say what she was thinking. Some friendships were stronger than any blood relation. They had their own unique sisterhood.

"I thought we were having a relaxing girls' night in." Simone set the headband on the sofa beside her and reached for her wineglass on the side table. "I can't relax wearing that and I most definitely cannot relax if you have us helping you put up Christmas decorations the day before Halloween."

Violet slipped around the corner into the narrow hallway and carried in a tote, then she went back and forth until she'd pulled in the other six.

"Okay, we love you, but even I need to step in here." Robin came to her feet and glanced around. "You are aware you live in about a one thousand square foot space and you have enough decorations for more than double that size? And you don't even have the tree out yet, which will take up even more room."

"Trees," Violet corrected. "I've decided to put up three this year."

"We rest our case," Simone added.

Violet plucked the lid off one tote and squealed at

her beloved white shimmery snowflakes, which she suspended from her arched doorways.

"No negativity, please," she told her friends as she started pulling out the décor. "You don't have to help if you don't want, but don't bash the most wonderful time of the year."

Simone straightened out her legs and sighed. "I'll just watch if it's all the same. You know I get twitchy if I put up anything before Thanksgiving, even if it's in someone else's house."

Violet shook her head. "I don't even know how we've remained friends."

"Because I ply you with raspberry macarons that make you weep."

Simone Adams owned Mad Batter, honestly the best bakery Violet had ever encountered. The place was slammed at any given time and to get a wedding cake from Simone would require getting on the list nearly a year in advance. After she won twenty thousand dollars on the popular TV show *Bring the Dough*, her business skyrocketed.

Robin shifted around to face Simone. "Did you bring macarons?"

"'Fraid not. But I am working on a new flavor for the holidays. I'm thinking one with an espresso, caramel blend and a spin on my vanilla bean with a little champagne in the filling. I promise to let you two be my tasters."

Robin lifted her glass in a mock cheers. "Sign me up for that."

Violet popped the lids off all of the totes because she had to find her garland first. The main rule of decorating was to layer and always start at the bottom or the base. She needed her window and fireplace garland. Not that she had a real fireplace, she only had a faux façade she'd purchased at an estate sale a couple years ago. She'd promptly put it in the space between her two windows overlooking the alley behind her shop.

One day, she vowed, she'd have a big traditional Southern home with multiple fireplaces and a curved banister leading to the second story. There would be lots of porch space on both levels of the home, and her children and husband would help her decorate and bake cookies. She thought she'd be in that position by now, considering she was thirty-three, but it was good to have goals. Family life wasn't for everyone, and she appreciated that her friends actually didn't want that familial lifestyle… but Violet dreamed of the future.

"She's doing it again."

Violet nestled a swag of greenery onto her window ledge and laughed at Robin's whispered statement. "I can still hear you and I was only daydreaming a little."

"Are we ready for these next two months?" Simone asked. "I'm afraid this will be our last girls' night until after the new year."

"Business is booming." Robin curled her feet beneath her on the sofa. "The Tinsel Tour alone is keeping me busy with all the fresh wreaths you requested."

Robin Foster owned Boulevard Bouquet, only the best florist in the entire state. Well, maybe not the entire state, but at least the tri-county area. She was the go-to for all things horticulture and outdoorsy. She could whip up an arrangement worthy of a royal wedding and never chip her signature pink polish.

"You know I appreciate how hard you work behind the scenes for me." Violet reached for her wineglass from the end table. "And, don't shoot me, but I need to add twenty more evergreen garlands." She cringed and shut her eyes, ready for the backlash.

"Already done," Robin laughed. "You think I order conservatively when it comes to you and Christmas? I actually have thirty more bundles coming in and I knew if you didn't ask for them, you'd still find a way to use every bit."

Violet relaxed and focused on her friend. "You know me so well."

Robin adjusted her headband and shifted on the sofa. "How's the chocolate walk menu looking, Simone?"

"Overwhelming at the moment, but nothing a ton of extra hours can't make up for. You know I do my best work last minute and my team is used to me." Simone groaned and dropped her head back. "Ugh. I just remembered the newspaper asked for an exclusive on Monday morning. I don't know how that slipped my mind."

"That's wonderful," Violet exclaimed. "I'm sure it will be front page, which will only help push those ticket sales for the events this season."

Not to mention help aid in a little surprise she hadn't told them about yet. Violet was so eager to tell them the exciting news, but she wanted to let the news naturally fall into the conversation.

Peach Grove was about to become a bit more popular, and Violet knew her friends would be thrilled…once they got over the shocking announcement.

In the not so distant past, their quaint area had become almost a ghost town. Businesses had closed, families had moved to larger cities to restart their lives. But Violet, Simone, and Robin grew up here, they loved this place, and slowly but surely they were breathing new life back by using their individual talents.

They'd each taken affordable, run-down buildings and started their businesses and saved money by living in the lofts above. Little by little, with word of mouth and the power of social media, plus Simone's television debut, their shops grew bigger than any of them expected. Weddings were the leading draw and the ladies realized they all complemented each other in that market. They often did cross-promoting and planned marketing strategies together to pull in even more brides.

Three years ago, Violet brought back the Tinsel Tour, a festive, fun tour of the old town mansions that was founded by William Jackson fifty years ago. So this year was a major milestone and she intended to go all out... even more than usual.

Violet had always loved the annual event when she'd been a kid, wondering what it would be like to grow up and actually call one of those places her own. But now, she got to decorate them and set the stage to launch Peach Grove's Christmas season.

Her seasonal Christmas shop, Yule Sleigh Me, was the perfect opportunity to use her creative skills and assist others in making their homes beautiful or finding that perfect gift.

"Make sure to talk up the tickets for the tour and the walk since the proceeds will go back to the city for that new park for the kids," Violet reminded her. "Oh, and if you could name-drop William Jackson, that would be great. His passing is a huge void to the community, but his home will still be on the tour."

She hoped. She'd yet to speak to William's grandson, who was now the new owner. Granted the man would have to actually come to town for Violet to speak to him because her phone calls had gone ignored, as had her emails and the save-the-date cards she'd mailed.

"I haven't seen Brady Jackson in years," Simone said, picking up her headband and twirling it enough to make the little bells jingle. "Not since our third and final date when we realized we had nothing in common and he seemed offended that I was a vegetarian."

Violet nearly snorted wine out of her nose. "You didn't tell him on the first two dates?"

"It never came up." Simone defended herself with a defensive huff. "The first date was a charity event we met at and the second was a movie so I had popcorn and Milk Duds. The third, he picked me up and we went to a steakhouse. I nearly ended things right there, but I de- cided to go in. When I got a salad and a side of fries he wasn't impressed. Which was fine, I wasn't impressed with how much he talked about his work, spreadsheets, and all the hours he spent in the office. Honestly, I'm surprised we made it three dates."

"There must've been one redeeming quality," Robin suggested.

Simone shrugged. "He was a pretty good kisser, but we didn't do anything beyond that."

"Well, I'm not looking to kiss him or anything else." Violet swirled the final drink and tossed it back. "I just need to know when I can get in to decorate and if he'll be around for the tour or if I can get a key."

Really, this was cutting it close. As the date closed in, Violet found herself growing quite twitchy. Hadn't he received the save the date back in August? Seriously. This was not a surprise she was springing on him. His grandfather started this entire thing, for pity's sake. You'd think the grandson of the town's equivalent of a patriarch would want to participate.

"Good luck." Simone snickered. "If he's anything like he used to be, I'm sure he'll send his assistant to handle the house and talk with you. And I wouldn't hold my breath on getting that key."

Violet didn't care at this point who she dealt with or who let her inside, so long as the Jackson mansion remained the last stop on the tour. Between William's passing just a few months ago and the fiftieth anniversary, this home was more important than any other.

Every estate had its own character and charm, but there was something about William's that had always tugged at Violet. Maybe it was the history, maybe it was the second-story balcony that stretched the length of the home and matched the grand porch. The tree-lined drive that provided a canopy of shade from the century-old oaks only added to the magnetism.

"We've lost her again," Simone whispered.

"Is she ever really here?" Robin laughed. "Nobody daydreams like Violet."

Violet rolled her eyes. "I can hear you guys, you know? I'm excellent at multitasking."

She turned to face all of the open totes and grabbed a bundle of gold flowers she always used to decorate her tiny breakfast table. She plucked one flower from the bundle and crossed the space to shove it behind Simone's ear.

"If you won't wear the headband, at least do something festive," Violet complained. "You're sucking the fun out of my apartment."

Simone laughed and tapped the flower. "I'll take this over that headband any day."

With her friends plied with their first glass of wine and all in good moods, Violet couldn't hold in the news anymore.

Waving a pair of gold candlesticks in the air, Violet cleared her throat. "Okay, so I have a major announcement. It might add to the stress of the season. We will have to all pitch in and do extra work, maybe even pull in some others to make everything flawless, but I think it's spectacular and I hope you guys—"

"What is it?" Simone yelled.

Robin laughed and held up her hands. "Why do I always have to play referee with you two. Simone, just let her ramble, she'll get around to it. Violet, spit it out before Simone explodes."

Violet bounced on her feet and clutched the candlesticks close to her chest as if she could hold on to this magical moment. An announcement of this magnitude couldn't be given while seated.

"Oh, this must be good." Robin's smile widened. "You're getting extra dramatic."

"You mean there's a time she's calm?" Simone asked.

Violet crossed her tiny living area and came to stand in front of the window. "Okay, so I got a call today that had me a little nervous at first, but the more I think about this idea, the more excited I'm getting."

"And the call was from?" Simone asked, motioning for Violet to get on with it.

"You're not going to believe this." Violet couldn't believe it herself, but she was over-the-moon excited…and a little terrified. "*Simply Southern Magazine*."

Robin's eyes widened. "What for?"

Violet squealed and Simone groaned. "Oh, no," her friend said. "No, no, no."

With a nod, Violet went on. "Oh, yes. They want to do a feature article about Peach Grove and our holiday events. And…"

Simone narrowed her eyes. "And what? Don't make me stab you with that reindeer headband."

Violet twisted her mouth and muttered, "They might want to interview each of us about our roles and our businesses."

Robin's laughter filled the living area and Simone simply fell back against the couch with her eyes closed. Her friends' reactions were exactly what Violet had expected, so at least she was somewhat mentally prepared.

Simone held up her hands. "Wait. How much time do we have to prepare for this? Because I have a couple of weddings coming up before I can start work on the chocolate walk menu."

Violet paced in her living area. "Well, they would like to come in two weeks so they can get the magazine to publication in time, but I told them we couldn't possibly have things set up by then."

"Well, that's something," Simone stated. "What did they say?"

Violet paused and cringed. "That they're coming anyway and plan on documenting the process."

Simone and Robin stared at each other, then back to Violet. From their wide eyes and gaping mouths, she had to assume that's the exact look she had when first presented the idea.

"This will be fun," she assured them. "Trust me."

Chapter Two

*It's all fun and games until Santa
checks the naughty list.
* Violet Calhoun*

Brady Jackson gripped his steering wheel and waited for the anxiety to subside. His boss told him once he got out of the city, he'd relax and not worry so much.

Well, Brady had been gone for three hours and as his headlights slashed across the large wooden sign that welcomed him to Peach Grove, he had more stress now than when he was in his Atlanta office. At least there he knew what was happening, but he had no clue what he'd do when he didn't head to Myers & Myers Law Firm first thing Monday morning.

Not only was he not going to be in the office that was practically his second home, he also wouldn't be volunteering at the planetarium that meant so much to him. A niggle of guilt crept up, but there wasn't much he could do about his circumstances right now.

Soon, he vowed. He would be back in Atlanta and back to everything that was his norm. He didn't do well with change and he sure as hell didn't do well with being displaced.

Peach Grove was the last place he wanted to be. Other than his grandfather's funeral a few months ago, Brady hadn't been back in about three years. He used to come every summer and spend time with his grandfather, but then college entered the picture, so did girls, one year rolled into another and the visits grew farther and farther apart until he was hired on at the law firm and devoted every waking minute to advancing his career.

While his grandfather was proud of him, Brady still had guilt about not coming around more, but nothing could change the past. His grandfather was gone and Brady had to push forward with his own life and attempt to salvage the career he might have destroyed.

Brady's parents had moved to the west coast when he'd graduated high school. Other than having William Jackson in his life, Brady wasn't much in with the whole family scene. Unfortunately, that's exactly the vibe this cozy town rippled of. There were no traffic lights, only stop signs, and if you pulled up at the same time as someone else, someone always waved the other person. Everybody either knew everybody or they were related.

In Atlanta, the drivers were a tad more aggressive and would honk and keep driving before letting you go first.

Lately, the stress load at work had been rising, which combined with the death of his grandfather, until Brady finally exploded on another lawyer representing his client's ex…in front of the judge, no less.

So, here he was "relaxing" for the next several weeks. Two months to be exact. He was ordered not to return until after the first of the year. But at least he hadn't been fired, so there was a bit of a silver lining, right?

He hated that his clients were being turned over to his colleagues, but that was nobody's fault but his own. He was furious with himself for not being able to control his temper. Beyond that, though, he was disappointed in himself for letting his current clients down…for letting himself down.

Brady turned up Peach Tree Lane, the picturesque tree-lined street that led to the nearly two-hundred-year-old home. Even with the long, wide driveway, Brady spotted the porch lights gleaming up ahead, almost calling him home. He didn't want to be here, not just because of the whole mess with his work and the fact he hated being away, but because of all of the memories that were waiting on him at this property.

When he'd come for the funeral, he hadn't stayed overnight and he hadn't gone back to the house. He'd left the cemetery and gone right back to Atlanta. Saying goodbye was something he wasn't ready for, so he didn't.

Yet here he was on a forced vacation and he'd had nowhere else he really needed to be. There was still so much to be done at the plantation home and with all this time on his hands, he guessed this was as good a place to stay for two months as any.

Brady had kept the utility bills paid on the home that had been willed to him, and now he had to figure out what to do with the place and all of the contents inside. Clearly he didn't need a mansion, let alone one so far from his job where he was still hoping he could make partner.

Okay, so that hope was a bit dimmer now that he'd been forced out for the next several weeks, but Brady wasn't a quitter. Yes, this was a major setback, but that didn't mean this was the end.

Brady pulled the car to a stop and killed the engine. First thing tomorrow morning he'd call a local Realtor and discuss putting the house on the market. If he didn't just jump in and get it done, he never would.

There went that damn guilt again.

He had no clue what his grandfather would've wanted done with the house. Likely he would've wanted it to stay in the family and keep that rich history alive and well with the Jackson name, but considering Brady's parents were divorced and his father was off traveling with his new girlfriend and Brady wasn't married, the chances of that happening were nil.

Deep in Brady's heart he knew William Jackson would've wanted Brady to keep this home, but Peach Grove wasn't the place Brady wanted to set roots. He had a life in Atlanta he was already itching to get back to.

Brady grabbed his suitcase from the back of his SUV and headed up onto the wide porch. The same sturdy wicker rockers were stationed between each window down either side from the front door. The fat potted plants on the edge near the steps were empty when they'd always been bursting with fresh blooms. No lights came from inside the home and he knew the second he opened that door, nostalgia would smack him in the face and he'd have to deal with his grief at some point.

But not right now.

Brady took a seat in the closest rocker and rested his hands between his knees. From the glow of the porch lights, he could make out the old tire swing swaying from the tall, strong oak. He could practically see a young Brady laughing and begging his grandfather to keep pushing.

How long ago was that? Thirty or more years, but it seemed like a lifetime. One summer Brady was carefree and running around this estate like he owned it. Now, well, he did own it, but he didn't want it and he certainly wasn't carefree.

Brady eased back in the rocker and attempted to do just what his boss demanded...relax.

This was going to be a long two months.

The murmuring of a female voice jerked Brady from his sleep. He pushed up from the oversized sofa in the front sitting area and raked a hand over his face.

Sunlight spilled through the tall, narrow windows and slanted onto the hardwood floor. He glanced around and realized he'd fallen asleep in his clothes after he'd managed to get inside yesterday evening. Pretty much this was the only room he'd stopped in because it was right off the front door, it held the majority of his memories, and he'd been utterly exhausted. Other than the briefcase by the couch, his suitcases were still out in the car.

Laughter filtered in from outside. Who the hell was here? And on a Saturday morning? Not what he wanted to deal with right now...or ever. Had trespassers been an issue since the place had been empty for a few months? The lawn crew he'd hired to maintain the yard came every Wednesday, not on the weekends.

Burglars didn't usually stand out in front of homes and joke, though. Nobody knew he was in town, so there shouldn't be visitors.

Brady came to his feet and stretched, realizing quickly he was too damn old to be sleeping on a sofa. He'd left that behind in law school.

As he headed to the foyer, Brady glanced to his wrinkled dress shirt and dress pants. Oh, well, at least he'd taken his tie and shoes off before he fell face-first into the couch.

Brady unlocked the door and jerked it open to find a lady chatting on her cell. She wore a pair of jeans and a green T-shirt and...

Was that a reindeer headband?

Wait, wasn't today Halloween? Brady knew he wasn't that overworked and stressed that he would be hallucinating. And he certainly wasn't exhausted enough to ignore the way that denim hugged her curves.

"Oh," Miss Headband exclaimed when her eyes landed on him. "I didn't know anyone was here."

Brady took a step farther onto the porch and shielded his eyes from the morning sun. "So you typically trespass on private property?"

She adjusted her headband and excused herself from whoever was on the other end of that call before sliding her cell in her back pocket. She looked familiar, but he couldn't place a name.

"Brady Jackson." She smiled wide as she marched up onto the porch like she owned the place. "I'm Violet Calhoun, I was a good friend of William's. I've been trying to get in touch with you for a while now."

Oh, yes. He knew her name from his grandfather and recalled seeing her here and there when he'd been in town years ago and at the funeral.

He also had become very familiar with the name due to her umpteen calls lately. He'd been too busy to listen to her seventeen voicemails—something about the holiday tour and other things that were totally irrelevant to his life at this point.

"It's Halloween." The words slipped out of his mouth before he could even think. "What's with the headband?"

With a beaming smile that stirred things inside him that didn't need stirred, she tapped the side of the reindeer antler. "I'm the events coordinator for the Tinsel Tour. That's the whole reason I've been trying to get in touch with you. I used to work with your grandfather on the tour, but since his passing, I'm in charge of the entire event."

Brady crossed his arms and stared at her. It was Halloween and she was already discussing Christmas? Yeah, the tour did take time to set up, he'd heard his grandfather discussing that enough, but William Jackson would've never been seen in a tacky accessory in his charge to get the ball rolling on the event.

"Didn't you get the save-the-date postcard I sent here back in August?" she asked.

Considering he also had a cleaning service come every few weeks to keep the place maintained and get the mail, tossing what looked like junk, no, he hadn't gotten that.

"Must've slipped through the cracks," he replied.

With a deep sigh, Violet pushed a dark red curl back up into the pile of hair on her head. He wasn't quite sure what was holding all of that up other than that ridiculous headband.

"Okay, well, you're here now and—" Her eyes raked over him. "Did I wake you?"

"Yes." Why lie? Maybe she'd take pity and leave.

"Do you usually sleep in a suit?"

Brady held out his hands and looked down. "It's a dress shirt and pants."

"Do you have a matching jacket to those pants?" she asked.

"Yes."

"Then it's a suit."

Brady gritted his teeth. Why was he arguing with a woman wearing a reindeer on her head?

"Anyway," she went on before he could speak. "Since I have you here, we need to get started right away on the decorating for the tour."

Violet went on, pointing to the windows, the columns, the porches. Her hands waved in a flurry at the mention of greenery, lighting, ribbons. Something about a theme and the six-foot-tall nutcrackers she'd found to flank the main entryway.

"And that's just the exterior. Now, don't worry, we only do the main floor, so upstairs doesn't need touched."

His mind was spinning and she was rolling over him like a tornado.

Violet clasped her hands and turned that megawatt smile his way. She'd be a beautiful woman if you could get beyond the holiday obsession and if he were looking for a distraction. He couldn't and he wasn't.

"Let's go inside and I can walk you through that."

Brady held up his hands. "Hold up, Blitzen. We're not going inside or discussing more decorating. This house won't be on the tour this year."

She stared for a second before she busted out laughing and swatted his shoulder like he'd just made the funniest joke.

"Of course it is," she volleyed back. "William prided himself on having his home being the last on the tour. He loved having people come through, and this is the fiftieth anniversary since the tour was started—you know, by your grandparents."

Yeah, he was well aware who started the Tinsel Tour, but he didn't have time or the energy to deal with an overly dramatic, crazed woman. He had a job to save, a house to sell, and memories to bottle up to last the rest of his life.

He wondered if he stayed away a few weeks and ended up back in Atlanta a little early, if Frank Myers would have cooled off and let him come back. It was worth a shot. Brady couldn't imagine staying in this big, quiet house for two months. His sanity simply wouldn't stand it.

"Listen, Violet, I appreciate all the work you put into what I'm sure is a fabulous event—"

"Don't patronize me," she interrupted. "This year, more than any other, is important and the Jackson home must be part of the tour. Not only is it tradition, the money from the ticket sales is going to fund the new children's park."

"I'll write a check."

Was she not listening? He wasn't going to be steam-rolled into this. Traditions weren't set in stone and they could actually be changed. If this was such an important year, maybe now was the time for a change. Why not start fresh with something else and leave him out of it?

"We will gladly accept your donation," she told him. "But our schedule is set and this home is on the itinerary."

Brady raked a hand over his jaw, the stubble bristling against his palm. He hadn't even been in town twelve hours and already had a new headache to add to his others.

"I'm selling." There, that should shut her up. "The home will be in the hands of the Realtor and hopefully under contract in a month, so there's no way it can be included."

Violet gasped and took a step back. Her eyes darted over his shoulder to the house in question and he could swear she'd gotten paler. What did she have invested in this place? Why would she care so much? The plantation hadn't been in her family for generations.

Every single time he thought of that, he had a pit in his stomach. He shouldn't sell, but in reality he knew there was really no other choice. Times changed and so did people. It was time for a new family to take over.

"Sell the house," she repeated on a whisper as her gaze shifted back to him. "But, why? This is your family's home and it's…well, it's magnificent."

Yes, it was both of those, but what would he do with a home of this size and in this town? Obviously she wasn't happy with the news and part of him believed that her despair didn't completely revolve around the tour.

"I have my reasons." None of which were her concern. "So as you can see, putting the home on the tour is impossible."

In a split second, she went from upset to steely. Those shoulders squared, she adjusted her headband, and she stood directly in front of him as if she could possibly match his size and stature.

"Well, I'm sure we can work something out. Give me the name of your Realtor. Everyone in town knows how important the tour and the rest of our town's festivities are, so I know they'll work with me."

Okay, time to close out this conversation that was literally going nowhere. The only thing progressing here was his damn headache.

"I'm not trying to be rude, but you have to respect my wishes. My grandfather would want me to do what was best with this house and my lifestyle above what the town would want."

Her eyes narrowed. He'd thought for sure that bit about his grandfather would sway her. Clearly she knew William well and respected him, but Brady wasn't convincing her.

No matter. He still wasn't caving and letting a crew of elves get into this house and decorate from top to bottom and inside out, no matter how attractive this woman was.

Attractive? Well, yeah. He couldn't deny that mass of red hair was striking, and her face, void of makeup with an all-natural girl-next-door vibe going on, was a refreshing change, but the lack of sleep and mounted stress was clearly messing with him.

"William would've wanted you to carry on the tradition he and your grandmother started. They didn't put all that work into it just to have it all end one day." She reached into the pocket of her jeans and pulled out a card. "Think about what I said and get me the name of the Realtor you choose, then call me. I know we can work this out for the good of the town and to benefit the children's park."

Brady took the card without looking down. Violet offered a smile, or a sneer, he couldn't really tell, before she spun on her heel and marched back toward her silver Jeep. She didn't glance back, didn't argue any more, she simply got in her vehicle and pulled down the drive.

He stood there for a moment, even after she'd turned onto the road and out of sight, and wondered what the hell had just happened. Did she think she'd won this battle?

Glancing down to the card, he noted her name in gold script. Beneath her name he read her title, EVENTS CO-ORDINATOR, which seemed like such a blanket term because this woman clearly had so many other qualities: pushy, demanding, determined.

The colorful flowers around the border seemed to fit

her—bright and wild. The slogan beneath her name had him torn between laughing or groaning.

Party woes? Hire a pro!

Brady had a sinking feeling this wasn't the last he'd seen, or heard, from Violet Calhoun.

Chapter Three

Always jingle all the way...
Nobody likes a half-assed jingler.
* Violet Calhoun

"You didn't tell me how arrogant he was."

Violet drove through downtown Peach Grove, heading to her shop and chatting with her bestie.

"Who?" Simone asked.

"Brady Jackson. I just had a run-in with him."

"I didn't know he was in town."

Violet spotted Mr. Banks, the oldest man in town, as she came to a stop sign. He waited to cross the street and she waved him on. He stepped down, leading with his cane in one hand and his dog leash in the other. Mr. Banks walked his old sheepdog every single morning and the man was like a staple in town. He'd been a good friend of William's, and Violet smiled as he nodded a thanks to her once he got to the other side.

"Oh, he's here all right," Violet said, as she moved through the intersection. "And he's a grouch. I would be, too, if I slept in a suit."

"What?"

Violet sighed. "Nothing. Listen, he's adamant that the

home not be on the tour and he's putting it up for sale. Can you believe that?"

"Selling the house? I didn't see that coming. Did he say why?"

"Not really. I got the impression he just doesn't want it, but he didn't really offer an explanation." Violet pulled into her parking spot behind her building and shut off her car. "I need to figure out a way to get him to let me keep the house on the tour."

"Did you tell him about *Simply Southern*?" Simone asked.

"No. I was hoping he'd just be nice without me groveling about what a bind I'd be in without the grand home of the man who started this whole thing."

Simone laughed. "Well, you might have to pull out the pouty face or flirt or something. Wait, no. Don't flirt. I don't even think that would work with him. If he's the same as he was years ago, he eats and breathes work."

So he was married to his job. She could adjust to that mindset, she just needed to regroup. She was a business-woman, after all.

"Then I'll simply appeal to his business side," she stated. "Money speaks to most people, right?"

The mere thought that the Jackson mansion wouldn't be on the tour never crossed her mind so the wind had been knocked out of her, that's all. Violet certainly wasn't done fighting.

"I'll figure out what magic I can do," Violet added. "I'll let you get back to work and see you tonight at the party. Love ya."

"Love you."

Violet disconnected the call and grabbed her purse from the passenger seat. The crisp morning was warming up with the sun beaming down. She had multiple calls to make to area homeowners to confirm their scheduled days and times for decorating. This was by far her busiest time of year, but also her favorite.

There was something so magical about Christmas, like regular everyday problems ceased to exist, even if for a short time. People seemed happier, kids were always smiling, families spent more time together.

She wanted that one day. A family, a big house to fill with memories and love. Her own childhood was filled with love and fun times. Her parents may have divorced when she was only fifteen, but they did love each other… they just weren't in love and felt it best to go their separate ways.

Violet let herself into the back of her building and keyed in the security code before flipping on all the lights. She skirted around the totes of Christmas décor, nutcrackers, giant ornaments for the Mason estate, and other finds she'd been hoarding since last Christmas. She also had a couple of storage buildings the city graciously donated, plus the homeowners had their own special treasures they incorporated into the displays.

Tradition was so important to this town and these people. There had to be a way to get Brady to see that. This wasn't just her being difficult. She wanted to keep this special tradition alive for as long as possible.

After unlocking the front door of Yule Sleigh Me, Violet adjusted the little elf holding the open sign in the window. As she started up the espresso machine, Burl Ives's "Holly Jolly Christmas" rang out from her cell.

Violet pulled her phone out and spotted her mother's name. "Hey, Mom. What's up?"

"Honey, do you have time to chat this morning? I

know you're super busy and I don't want to be in the way, but—"

"I'm never too busy for my mother," Violet interrupted. "I'm working in my store today and I'm separating things in the back room for the tour. Is something wrong?"

"Wrong? Oh no. Everything is great. I'll tell you when I get there."

Her mother disconnected the call and Violet stared at her cell. Lori Calhoun was not a morning person. Ever. So something had her up and chipper this early in the day.

Curious about her mother's sudden burst of enthusiasm, Violet made herself a cup of espresso and added a dash of cream and chocolate shavings on top. Might as well kick off her busy day the right way. She had much to fit in before she could head upstairs and get into her stocking costume.

As eager as she was for the holiday festivities coming just around the corner, Violet was excited for tonight. Any reason to dress up in costume was fine by her. Plus, the carnival was a great way to show appreciation to the community. All firefighters, EMTs, police, active and former military, were all admitted free of charge.

Violet loved that her town was growing, and doing more and more things like this was only helping outsiders see that Peach Grove was the up-and-coming town she and her friends longed for it to be.

Violet took her frothy drink to the checkout counter in the corner and set it on her Christmas wreath coaster. She booted up her laptop and then took a sip, welcoming the caffeine and sugar rush.

She spent the next half hour scrolling through the list of homeowners and making notes on various themes and questions she needed to ask each one. She'd worked with them all before and was anxious to do so again. There was only one new home added to the list and she would have to set up a time to go speak with them in person and get a more detailed plan in place.

Just as she reached for her cell, the front door opened and her mother breezed in.

"It is a glorious morning," she sang, holding up a familiar pale blue box from Simone's bakery, Mad Batter.

Violet came to her feet and rounded her desk. "I don't care what's in there, I'm just happy you brought me something."

"I grabbed cream horns for now and got you three macarons for later." Her mother leaned forward and kissed Violet on the cheek. "This morning calls for a celebration."

Violet took the box and turned to set it on her desk before focusing back on her mom. "What on earth has gotten into you today?" she asked. "I've never seen you so happy and...well, bubbly."

Her mother's smile widened. "Well, I have some news. I hope you're going to be just as thrilled."

"What is it?" Violet found herself smiling because if her mother was this happy, it must be something life changing.

Her mom popped up her left hand and wiggled her fingers—the light bounced off a rock that had to be several carats. Violet squealed and grabbed her mother's hand.

"Mom! This is...this..."

Her mother laughed. "I know. I was speechless, too when he asked me. So, I guess I'm getting married."

Instant tears pricked Violet's eyes. Her mother seemed

so, so happy and this was exactly what she deserved. A second chance at a happily ever after was something true fairy tales were made of.

"Are you okay with this?" she asked.

Violet wrapped her arms around her mom and sniffed. "More than okay. This is the best news I've had in a long time."

Her mother eased back and squeezed Violet's shoulders. "I didn't think you'd be opposed, but I really wanted your blessing. Can you believe I'm marrying the mayor? I guess that will make me the First Lady of Peach Grove."

Violet laughed and turned toward the counter. She opened the box and pulled out two cream horns, handing one to her mother.

"Do you want coffee or an espresso?"

"Coffee, please. I feel like we should celebrate with champagne or something, though."

Violet placed her pastry on a napkin at the corner coffee bar and fired up the Keurig. She grabbed a mug with her Christmas shop logo and put it under the drip. "I will take you and Porter out to dinner to celebrate properly. Just tell me when you're free to go."

"Actually, that's another reason I wanted to tell you in person," her mom said as she moved in beside her. "I have a huge favor to ask."

There was nothing Violet wouldn't do for her mother. "Name it."

"I want you to plan my wedding."

Violet nearly screamed. "Of course I will! This will be my best work yet. So are you thinking summer? Because the girls and I are talking of doing a Bridal Expo at the park near the pond with the gazebo. It just screams romantic."

Her mom's pink glossy lips twisted. "Well, we wanted to be married sooner than summer."

"Spring weddings are gorgeous, too. Not too hot. Are you wanting inside or out? Have you thought of the venue? I know magnolias are everywhere down here, but they're such a classic flower."

The coffee stopped and Violet added the sugar-free vanilla syrup that her mother loved. She picked up the mug and turned to her mom.

"We were thinking even sooner," her mom said with a slight wrinkle of her nose.

Violet nodded. "Oh, Valentine's Day! That would be perfect. You've waited a long time to find the love of your life."

"Honey, I know you're swamped, but we'd like to be married on Christmas Eve."

Violet stilled, her words caught in her throat.

Christmas Eve? In the midst of her busiest season, the one she planned for the other eleven months out of the year, she was to plan the most important day of her mother's life?

Not only that, Christmas Eve was less than two months away. How could she possibly plan her mother's special day in such a short time?

Violet's grip slipped and the mug shattered onto the floor. Could her life get any more chaotic right now?

"Oh, Vi." Her mother sprang into action and ran to the bathroom, rushing back with a roll of paper towels. "I didn't mean to shock you. I know it's the worst season to ask anything of you—"

"No, no. It's fine. I'll be fine. Everything will be just... fine."

Her mother squatted to clean up the mess, and peered

up at Violet. "If you say fine again, maybe you'll start believing it. We can change the date, sweetheart. Don't stress."

Violet sighed and squatted down to pick up the shards. Her mother had finally found true love and Vi was being selfish. If the woman wanted to marry tomorrow morning, Violet would make it happen.

"I'm a jerk," she said as she placed the broken pieces in a pile to sweep. "I will create your dream wedding on any date you want."

Her mother's smile beamed once again. "I'll do anything I can to help, but since the entire town is so festive and beautiful, I didn't think there would be too much to do."

Violet nearly laughed, but refrained. The décor was only part of the wedding. There was food, flowers, venue, music, seating charts…the list continued to grow in her mind, but Vi kept everything to herself. She'd take on every chore to make her mother's day absolutely perfect and one she deserved.

"Have you talked to Dad yet?" Violet asked.

Lori gathered her wet paper towels and came to her feet. "I wanted to talk to you first. Your father and Tara will be happy for me. I think they knew this was coming."

Tara and Violet's father, Scott, had been married for nearly ten years. As odd as it sounded or appeared to outsiders, they all got along. There was no doubt in Violet's mind that her father and stepmother would be thrilled for Lori and Porter.

Once the mess was cleaned up, Violet started a new cup of coffee and picked up her cream horn. "Tell me how he proposed. I bet he did something romantic. Am I right? Please tell me he went all out."

Lori took a seat on one of the plush accent chairs by the coffee bar and clutched her mug. Violet had to admit the diamond looked amazing on her mother's well-manicured hand.

"He actually was pretty low-key," her mother admitted. "Which just embodies who we are. He made me dinner and afterward we were on his back patio on the porch swing. The sun had set, the stars and full moon were out. The night was perfect. I nestled against his side and we sat in silence. I realize now he was probably trying to come up with a way to ask, but all he said was that he wanted me to know how much he loved me and he also wanted to know how I felt about a name change. When I glanced up, he had the ring."

There were all types of engagements, and as far as this one went, there were no bells and whistles, but all that mattered was how her mother felt and how perfect she and Porter were together.

Violet didn't mention the whole magazine thing, not wanting to deter from her mother's exciting news. Besides, if Vi mentioned *Simply Southern*, then her mother would feel guilty about her wedding date and that's the last thing Vi wanted.

She'd tell her later and assure her everything was going to work out just fine—and it would, so long as Mr. Grinch got on board with the festivities.

Chapter Four

I'm going to go lie under the tree and remind my friends what a gift I am.
* Violet Calhoun

Maybe a human stocking wasn't the smartest costume she'd ever designed, but it was only for one night and Violet had to admit, this ranked up there with one of her more unique ideas.

She just wished she hadn't made the furry top so fluffy around her neck. The candy cane and teddy bear poking out the top were also quite annoying. At least she'd thought to pull her unruly curly hair up into a high ponytail.

"That costume is so you."

Violet spun around on her bright red stilettos and smiled as she took in the Jasmine costume. "Wowza. Simone, girl, you have been hiding that body under frumpy clothing."

Simone held out her arms, showing off the shimmery pale blue material that flowed around her hips and the bra top that fit perfectly for her new figure. Her giant gold hoops looked like a stark contrast against her dark, silky hair.

"I've been working my ass off, literally," Simone

laughed. "It's hell getting depression and gaining weight, but I'm back."

Her friend had struggled with the mental illness for several years. Violet and Robin never really knew what caused the sudden onset, but Violet was just glad her friend had a smile on her face again and had the confidence she used to. No matter her size, Simone should love herself as much as they all loved her.

"Have you seen Robin?" Simone asked, glancing around. "I figured she'd beat me here."

"Not yet." Violet smoothed the white fur from below her chin. "Remind me not to do this costume again. The fur is too much."

"What? Something festive is too much for you? I'm shocked."

Violet rolled her eyes. "Shut up," she laughed. "Listen, I have some little cards to pass out as reminders about the Tinsel Tour. I brought some for all of us to pass out."

Simone's eyes raked over Violet. "You have cards hidden in that stocking?"

Violet slid her hand into the side pocket and pulled out a handful. "I wouldn't make a costume without pockets. It's not like I can carry a handbag with this outfit."

"Handing out Christmas event cards at a Halloween party is a bit wrong," Simone stated, staring at the stack. "Besides, it's not like people don't know this tour exists. It's been in the town for forty-nine years."

"And this is the fiftieth," Violet agreed, taking her friend's hand and slapping some cards against her palm. "This is by far the most important one we've ever had. So humor me and let's chat up those ticket sales."

Simone sighed and shook her head. "I only do this because I want to help the children get their new park."

"And because you love me."

"You know I do," Simone added with a smile.

Violet glanced around the spacious park but didn't see any sign of Robin. There were so many costumes, some with masks and face paint, that Violet couldn't even identify everyone. Children ran around squealing with their bags, waiting on the trick-or-treat stations to open up.

As far as holidays went, Peach Grove did go all out to make the community feel involved and offer opportunities for everyone to mingle and socialize. Everyone here felt like family and even when new people moved to town or just passed through, the townsfolk always welcomed them with a warm smile.

There was something so cozy and charming about living in the South. Violet wouldn't trade it for anything. Peach Grove was the greatest place on earth if you asked her, not that she'd traveled much. She never had a desire to go anywhere else.

"I'm sure she'll be here soon," Violet stated. "Let's go ahead and get to our spots so we're not mauled by children."

The first hour of the festival was the candy hop, with all local businesses set up to pass out candy or various treats.

This year Violet, Robin, and Simone opted to do a candy theme. Vi wanted it to be a gingerbread house, but after some persuasion from her friends, they swapped out the red and white pinwheels for pink and white with oversized colorful foam gumdrops leading up to their booth.

Simone was pulling out the specialty candies she'd made and bagged in little colorful bags when Robin breezed in, smoothing her hair back from her face.

"Sorry I'm late. I was in an accident."

Simone and Violet both stopped what they were doing.

"Are you all right?"

"What happened?"

Their questions came out at the same time, but Robin was nodding. "Yes, I'm fine. Still shaky, but I'm not injured. I would've been here an hour ago, but we had to call the police and file a report."

Violet took hold of Robin's hands. "Why don't you sit down. Simone and I can handle the rush here once we get started."

"No, really. I'm okay," Robin insisted. "But I did get to know Brady Jackson a bit more now."

Violet gasped. "You hit Brady Jackson?"

"He hit me," Robin countered. "Or, rather, his big fancy SUV hit mine."

"Was he injured?" Simone asked.

"No. He was backing out of Sinclair Realty and there were tree-trimming trucks in the way. He claims he didn't see me."

"Sinclair Realty?" Violet asked. "The nerve of that man."

What a jerk. Already talking to the Realtor? Why would he do such a thing? She'd flat-out told him she needed this house on the tour and she even told him to call her.

She did tell him to give her the name of a Realtor he might want to work with, but she hadn't heard a word from him.

Clearly Mr. Scrooge was more interested in the almighty dollar than heritage and tradition. Now Violet would have to stop by Sinclair Realty and have another visit with Brady Jackson.

"Oh, no," Simone whispered. "She's getting that crazed look again."

Violet blinked and focused back to her friends. "No. I'm not going to explode, not yet anyway. Let's get through this festival and then I'll revisit that idea. I need to speak with him before I decide how angry I should be."

Angry and disappointed. He could do whatever he wanted, but she wished like hell he'd reconsider.

"Brady doesn't know who he's up against," Robin said as she started filling the white trays with all of the treat bags. "He did seem rather sidetracked and put out that he was in an accident. He kept saying he didn't have time for this."

Simone snorted. "Sounds like the same Brady I dated. He doesn't make time for anything other than work."

"Well, he can work all he wants, so long as I can get in there and decorate," Violet stated. "But let's sort that out later. We're about to get bombarded with crazed kids waiting for their sugar high."

Over the next hour, Violet saw the cutest costumes: puppies, witches, astronauts, and some even came through with their dogs dressed up. As Robin and Simone passed out treats, Violet chatted with parents and slipped them the cards about the tour. Violet only felt a little guilty about advertising the tour when the main attraction was still so undecided.

Well, she decided the Jackson home was still a go, even though Brady wasn't quite on board yet.

"I believe that's the last of things." Robin stacked the empty trays on top of each other. "We are wiped out once again."

"And I'm out of cards," Violet said. "I think I might skip out early."

"Going to talk to Brady?" Simone asked with a quirk of her brow.

"I need to get on this before he puts that place on the market. If he could just wait until after the holidays," she told them. "I can't have our main attraction off the tour and not available when the journalists get here. Everything needs to be perfect and timing is absolutely everything right now."

"With or without the Jackson estate, the tour will be perfect like always," Robin assured her. "All of the homes are historical and lovely."

"They are," Violet agreed. "But they aren't the Jackson mansion. William Jackson started this tour nearly fifty years ago. How could that home not be part of the anniversary celebration?"

"Calm down," Simone muttered under her breath. "No need to get worked up here. Just go talk to him, but you can't attack him or irritate him."

Violet understood that and appreciated the advice. This was a business transaction, but at the heart of everything there were people and feelings and the spark of hope that this season brought every year to Peach Grove. How could the man not understand that?

Beyond all of that, how could he sell such a gorgeous home that had been in his family for generations?

As Violet headed to her car, swatting at the fur still tickling her chin, she realized she hadn't told her friends the good news about her mother getting engaged. She would have to call them later and fill them in. For now, though, she had a Grinch to face.

Brady was tempted to ignore that tap on his door, but considering his day had already gone to hell with the damage to his SUV, it couldn't get much worse.

The second he came down the wide curved staircase

and glanced out the etched sidelights of the front door, Brady realized his day could indeed get worse.

He wasn't in the mood for any type of visitor, let alone the chipper Christmas crew. And what the hell was she wearing?

Brady pulled in a deep breath, flicked the lock, and opened the door.

"You went to see Donna Sinclair when I specifically asked you to let me talk to the Realtor of your choice first?"

Brady didn't know whether to be annoyed at her rant and putting her nose in his business or to laugh at her trying to be angry while standing here dressed like an overgrown stocking.

He decided he could be both.

"You look ridiculous," he told her with a laugh, simply because he knew it would annoy her. "And what I do with this house is not your concern."

She crossed her arms over her chest, sending that ruffle of fur up toward her mouth where she had to swat it away. Brady had to bite the inside of his cheek to keep from laughing again. She didn't look too intimidating when she was fighting with her ridiculous costume.

"What the hell are you wearing anyway?" he asked.

"My Friday outfit."

Brady gripped the handle of the door and willed for patience. This woman could test him more than any other and in less time. Why was he even entertaining conversations with her?

"You missed the town Halloween festival," she informed him.

Well, that at least explained the getup. Leave it to Violet Calhoun to dress up as a Christmas item for a Halloween party. What was this holiday obsession?

"I don't do festivals or costumes," he stated. "Is there a purpose to your visit or did you just want to reprimand me for talking to Donna?"

"I want to know why you're so adamant about not letting this house be on the Tinsel Tour."

Because he didn't want strangers traipsing through to decorate and then more strangers coming through taking pictures and ogling his family's things. He didn't want to be here at all dealing with this estate and trying to figure out what to do with everything.

But it was all of the memories that he didn't want to deal with. He hadn't been ready for that. Each room, each piece of furniture or decoration told a story.

"Listen, I have quite a bit to do and the tour just doesn't fit into my schedule."

Violet dropped her arms and took a step toward him. Those bright blue flecks in her eyes captivated him for just a moment. He reminded himself he couldn't get sidetracked by a sexy woman with mesmerizing eyes. He was supposed to be focusing on decompressing and relaxing so he could go back fresh to the law firm and not verbally rip people's heads off.

"Your grandparents started this tour," she reminded him again, her voice low and almost threatening. "This is the fiftieth anniversary, plus all of the proceeds will go toward the new children's park. Added to all of that pressure, I have been informed that *Simply Southern Magazine* will be arriving in less than two weeks to do an article on this town, specifically this tour. Now, I'm done tiptoeing around this and I'm not afraid to beg."

A magazine? No wonder she was stressing. But these

were not his problems. If she wasn't so maniacal, she'd be pretty hot, even wearing a human-sized stocking.

"Listen," he started. "I appreciate the position you're in, and I even appreciate you trying to keep this tradition alive, but some things can't last forever."

She took another step toward him, closing the gap and fully invading his personal space. Brady stared into those deep blue eyes and wished like hell he could shake this pull toward her. He didn't have time for attraction or tours or anything else revolving around Violet Calhoun.

He just wanted to stay holed up in this house, figure out how to divide all the contents, and sell the place. Then he wanted to get back to work and he prayed the firm didn't decide to fire him before then.

"I'm not asking this tour to last forever," she defended. "I'm asking it to last as long as I'm in charge."

Silence settled between them. What could he say that hadn't already been said? Talking to Violet was like talking to a wall. This round and round was going absolutely nowhere.

"I have an idea." She took a step back and pulled in a deep breath, then swatted at that white fur once again. "You let me decorate the house for the tour, you will play nice with the guests coming through and the journalists from *Simply Southern*, and in turn I will help you sell this house."

Brady crossed his arms and contemplated her statement. "In theory that sounds perfect, but you can't guarantee this house will sell."

Violet laughed and shook her head. "Do you even know how much this home is coveted by the people in this town? If I had the money, I'd buy it today. Besides, I promise I can get this house sold in record time. Once the holidays are over, we will stage a grand open house party. I would love to stage this home to get ready to put on the market. I'm a master at preparation and staging. We will make it like a cocktail hour and—"

"What the hell are you talking about?" he asked.

"An open house party," she told him, like he was a complete moron. "You want to make it an event to drive more people. You can't just call it an open house. People need to see how they can entertain here because that's exactly what we need for people to give top dollar. Trust me, this is what I do. I make boring parties and events bigger than you can imagine. This is the perfect plan."

Someone with her experience could be useful in pushing this process through. Having it staged properly would help it sell faster, and if she was willing…

Was he seriously contemplating this? More to the point, was he seriously having a serious conversation with a woman wearing a Christmas stocking?

"Ah, you're silent," she said with a wide grin that punched his gut with a heavy dose of unwanted lust. "That means you're considering my plan."

"I'm just trying to figure out where I lost control," he admitted.

"You haven't lost control," she amended. "In fact, you can assist me in every aspect of the tour and the open house regarding your home. There's no reason we both can't get what we want out of this."

He highly doubted he'd come out on top here and after the holidays was too late. He wanted all of this wrapped up before he went back to Atlanta at the first of the year.

"You're thinking about it, aren't you?" she asked. "How about this? You take your time to think, and by take your time, I mean a day. I am still limited with everything that's going on."

Brady rubbed the back of his neck, instantly feeling that tension headache coming on. He was supposed to be relaxing, keeping those headaches and frustrations at bay. That last case of his nearly did him in. Aside from the fact he'd taken it much too personally, he'd exploded in a courtroom. If he ever wanted to make partner, or hell, even keep working as an attorney, he had to rein in those emotions and keep a professional face on at all times.

"Deal?" Violet prompted.

He refocused on those dark blue eyes that never wavered from him. Clearly she didn't back down when she was passionate about something, which was certainly a quality he could appreciate…but that didn't mean he had to like it.

Did anyone ever say no to this woman? She'd make a hell of an attorney.

Her cell chimed and somehow she procured the thing from a pocket. She had a damn pocket in this getup. She held up a finger and smiled as she answered her call.

Brady waited, still wondering how the hell she seemed to think she'd won this argument. He was a powerhouse lawyer who could stand up against anyone in and out of the courtroom. Yet somehow this petite woman with some Christmas vendetta had managed to overthrow all of his brain cells. Maybe it was that mass of dark red hair he actually liked, or maybe it was those sexy red heels. Either way, she was holding all the strings and he was letting himself get jerked around.

"I'm sorry," she told him, still holding her cell. "This is important. Just call me tomorrow and we'll discuss the tour and your listing. Thanks."

And with that, she let herself out of his house as she went back to her call.

He hadn't agreed to anything, yet the way she'd left things made it seem like they'd wrapped up this conversation into some tidy, neat package.

Raking a hand through his hair, Brady headed back toward the study where he'd been searching through his grandfather's things.

He'd wanted a distraction from sorting through old photos and memories, but he hadn't necessarily wanted another run-in with the confusing, albeit sexy, Violet Calhoun.

She'd be back, though, and he had to mentally prepare himself for that next run-in. So far he'd been here two days and had seen her as many times. If he was guessing, he'd say she'd be back tomorrow.

Brady cursed himself for that niggle deep inside him that anticipated her next visit.

Chapter Five

I'm dreaming of a wine Christmas.
* Violet Calhoun

"Would you just tell us the news already?" Simone begged for the fifth time in as many minutes.

Violet eyed the tray of various macarons and chose carefully. "Not until my mother gets here," she replied.

"Oh no. Are you pregnant?" Robin asked.

"What? No. Who would be the father?" Violet asked with a laugh. "The only action I get lately is when I accidentally lean against the washer while it's running."

Robin snorted and rolled her eyes. "You need to get out more. Hell, we all do."

"Then if this doesn't have to do with a man, what is the big news?" Simone finished piping the edge of a pale lavender cake. "We just saw each other last night at the festival. Did something happen between then and now?"

"Well, things unfold that need discussed in person," Vi stated, biting into a vanilla bean toffee macaron. "And you will be glad we did this in person. Trust me."

"Does this have anything to do with Brady Jackson?" Simone grumbled.

"No, though he is still a problem. I'm working around it, though."

"So you're still butting heads and the magazine people are coming next week," Robin stated. "Maybe you should just admit defeat, Vi. We have other areas that need our attention."

"The area that needs my attention is the Jackson mansion," she clarified. "Of all people, he should understand the importance of this."

"He should, but it sounds like he's still hardheaded," Simone mentioned. "Listen, you need a time frame. Like, if he doesn't cave by Friday you'll move on, or something like that."

Violet eyed the other macarons, but decided she better pace herself. The holiday season was long and she'd have many other opportunities to sample her friend's goodies. Besides, she'd just bought a killer white and gold dress that she wanted to wear for a Christmas party and she damn well refused to exchange it for a bigger size.

"Oh, I told him tomorrow was the deadline and then I left without giving him a chance to argue or come up with another ridiculous reason to be excluded."

"I'm sure that went over well," Robin laughed.

Simone finished piping lavender roses, and every time Violet watched her friend, she was so amazed at how flawless she made the job appear. Violet did good to make a Pop-Tart and not burn it. Though she wished she was better in the kitchen. At some point in her life she did want that family and she couldn't exactly afford takeout every night.

Maybe she'd marry a chef. Now that would be the ultimate fantasy. A sexy man in an apron making her favorite foods. Yeah, that's definitely the way she should go.

"We've lost her again," Robin whispered.

Violet laughed and grabbed another macaron. The hell with her waistline. She had elastic pants for back-ups. "You haven't lost me. But, circling back. I did tell Brady that I would personally stage the home and throw a lavish party for an upscale open house after the holidays. There's no way that house will stay on the market long, but showcasing just how grand the place is and how perfect it is for entertaining will hopefully help drive the price up and pique an interest in his greedy heart."

Simone set down her piping tube and stared across the large island. "You didn't."

"I did. Why? I thought it was a brilliant plan."

Simone shook her head. "Why would you purposely want to work with him on anything? The guy is a jerk. You shouldn't have to beg him to continue a tradition his own family started."

"I like to see the silver lining in everything," Violet told her. "If we're helping each other, then it's a win all the way around. I want that house and I'm not opposed to working harder for it. Besides, this would be my only chance to throw a party that grand in a place like that. I mean, I do events all over, but this will be my party and I—"

"We know," Robin chimed in. "You've lusted over that house for years."

"Who wouldn't?" Violet shrugged. "The place is something out of *Gone with the Wind*. It's the perfect Southern plantation with those old oak trees lining the drive. Those porches stretching across the first and second floors of the home. The gardens, the staircase."

"Stop daydreaming and let's focus," Simone scolded.

"When is your mother going to be here? Because I really want to know what this impromptu meeting is all about."

Violet couldn't contain her smile. "I swear, she'll be here any minute and the news will be worth the wait."

"Is she buying the Jackson mansion?" Simone asked.

"Not hardly, though that would solve all of my problems."

The back door of the bakery opened and Lori strolled in with a wide smile on her face and her hair still perfectly in place. Violet's mother might be well into her sixties, but could easily pass for twenty years younger. Vi only hoped she inherited those anti-aging genes.

"So sorry I'm late, girls." Lori hung her purse on the hanger just inside the door and turned to flash them a smile. "Oh, what do we have here, Simone? Whatever it is, I'll take it."

"I have some macarons if your daughter doesn't eat them all," Simone laughed and gestured toward the platter. "Vanilla bean and toffee, raspberry, pistachio, and a salted caramel."

"I'll have one of each." Lori crossed to the island and stared at the platter before reaching forward. "Now, let's see, which one—"

"Oh my word," Robin gasped. "Is that a giant rock on your very important finger?"

Lori held up her hand and wiggled her fingers. "It is!" she exclaimed. "Porter asked me to marry him the other night."

Simone and Robin both squealed and ran around the workspace to grab hold of Lori's hand.

"This is so exciting," Simone claimed as she wrapped Lori in a tight embrace. "Do you guys have a date yet?"

Violet's mother threw her a glance and smiled, then wrinkled her nose. "We do."

"Is there something wrong?" Robin asked.

"Nothing at all is wrong," Violet assured everybody. "Christmas Eve will make a stunning backdrop and the perfect day for a wedding."

Silence filled the room and Violet widened her eyes and gritted her teeth, silently staring at her friends to get them to agree with her. They all had to be on board with this to pull off her mother's much-deserved dream day.

"Of course it will be a wonderful day," Robin quickly agreed. "I can't wait to get started on the flowers. Have you given any thought to them?"

Lori shrugged. "I really want you girls to surprise me. I trust each of you and you all know my tastes. You're much better at making these decisions than I am. I mean, you do weddings all the time and this is my first real wedding. The first one was at the courthouse, so the only decision I made was which hand-me-down dress to wear."

Vi couldn't wait for her mother to begin this next chapter in her life. True, the timing would cause a little more chaos, but this was what Violet did. She made events come to life for her clients and her mother's wedding would be the most important job she'd ever have.

Switching into work mode, Violet leaned against the island and faced her mother. "I know you want us to just whip up something fabulous, and we will, but I think I can speak for each of us when I say we'd like just a little direction. Like, Simone can give you photos of five different cakes and you can tell her what you do and don't like about each one. And Robin can do the same with various arrangements."

Her mother pursed her pale pink lips and nodded. "I

can do that. Oh, girls, this is going to be so much fun. I do have two more favors to ask on top of everything else I'm asking from you."

Violet reached for her mom's hand and smiled. "Mom, we will do anything for you. Name it."

"Well, I'd love if we could all find a day to go dress shopping," she explained. "And I'd be so honored if you three would stand up with me. I realize I'm probably too old to have bridesmaids—"

Robin squealed. "Of course we will and you are definitely not too old for anything. This is your wedding, so do your day however you want."

Lori's eyes welled up and Violet wrapped her arms around her mom. This was going to be the best Christmas ever. The most magical, the most exciting, just the most everything.

"You guys are the absolute best," Lori sniffed. "I keep crying like an idiot, but I'm just so happy."

"And we're happy for you," Simone added. "We will make your day the best one of your life. You name it, and we can make it happen."

Violet absolutely loved her friends for always treating her mother like their own. There weren't many people who would want their mother as part of their friendship circle, but Vi always thought of her mom as one of her best friends. They'd never gone through that hatred phase so many teens go through. Lori had always been understanding and offering sound advice to a younger Violet. And the way Lori just clicked with Simone and Robin always made it easy for Violet to include her mother in everything.

"I know you are all busy with the chocolate walk and

the tour, so don't stress yourselves over my day. I will honestly be happy with anything you come up with."

"Don't forget the magazine," Simone added with a laugh that came out a little more crazed and stressed than humorous.

Lori's eyes widened as she turned toward Violet. "Magazine? What magazine?"

"You didn't tell her?" Simone accused. "*Simply Southern* is coming to Peach Grove to do an article on the three of us and the Tinsel Tour. They'll be here next week."

Lori gasped. "Oh, my word. I need to move the wedding."

"No, you don't," Violet ordered. "You're getting married on the day you want and that's the end of it. Everything will already be decorated for the occasion and we will take care of the rest. I promise, we're fine. There just might be cameras or a journalist following us around."

Robin laughed. "Great. Now I feel like I need to always have my hair fixed and makeup on."

"You're gorgeous the way you are," Simone told her friend.

Robin always had her hair in some wild bun on top of her head, but the messy look always worked for her and she was damn adorable.

"Your hair is the least of my worries with this tour and the interviews." Violet snagged one more macaron and vowed to make this one her last. Really this time. This was it. "If I can't get Brady to cooperate, I'll need to find another home to fill that slot and we've already gotten every historical house."

"Speaking of Brady," Simone stated, turning to Robin. "How are you after the accident? Sore at all?"

"Oh, no. Nothing was hurt."

"Accident?" Lori asked, concern lacing her voice. "What happened?"

Robin shook her head. "Nothing major. Brady backed into me yesterday, but there was minimal damage to my car, although his back end was damaged quite a bit."

"Well, I'm glad you're okay," Lori said. "Listen, I hate to run, but I'm supposed to meet Porter for a late dinner."

Violet hugged her mother. "Go, have fun. We'll start brainstorming on this perfect wedding."

Her mother pointed her finger and got that stern look. "Now, I mean it when I say don't put yourselves out too much. I love everything you guys do, so I'll be happy with anything."

"I want you beyond happy, Mom. It's the most important day of your life."

Her mother laughed. "Who would have thought I'd even be planning a wedding at my age. Shouldn't we just go to the courthouse or fly off to Vegas or something?"

"There's no age limit on a wedding, especially a second chance. Take it, make it what you want."

Violet smiled at Robin's advice. Vi couldn't have said it better herself.

Her mother gave each of her girls a kiss and swept out the back door.

"I'm so happy for her," Robin said once they were all alone again. "We do have our work cut out for us."

Violet pulled in a deep breath. "Guys, I know this is the worst timing, so I understand if you don't—"

"Not another word," Simone commanded with her hand up. "We will do anything for your mom, you know that. So let's focus and make this the best day ever for her."

Violet smiled. "We better get to work, then."

Chapter Six

All I'm saying is I rarely see a person crying and eating a Christmas cookie at the same time.
* *Violet Calhoun*

Brady stared down at the assortment of pastries and admired the blue-and-white-checkered decorative box from Mad Batter. Fancy, most likely costly, and he didn't even need to read the note to know who this care package came from.

Violet.

She was pulling out all the stops to get this house on the tour. He understood her reasoning, but couldn't she respect his wishes and his need to have some privacy?

They both had goals. Unfortunately, the goals took this home in opposite directions and considering he was the owner, he was going to have the final say.

Before Brady could think if he wanted to call and thank her for the box of treats or call and tell her to stop trying so hard, his cell rang. He pulled his phone from his pocket and glanced at a number he didn't recognize.

"Brady Jackson," he answered.

"Brady, this is Mick down at the body shop."

"Yes, Mick. How's my car coming?"

Because this replacement pickup truck wasn't really his style. The white bed didn't exactly match the black cab and the horn sounded like a dying cat. Not to mention the fact the damn thing didn't even have power steering.

"Well, there's a minor hiccup, but nothing to worry about."

Any hiccup, no matter how small, was something to worry about when it came to his SUV. He'd just bought that vehicle two months ago. Brady gripped the cell and stared up at the ceiling, looking for divine intervention or just some semblance of control that he'd somehow lost since coming into Peach Grove.

"So what's the problem exactly?" he asked.

"That part I ordered won't be delivered for four weeks."

Four weeks? Was the piece being brought in by horse and buggy or carrier pigeon?

Brady blew out a sigh and waited to respond as Mick went on.

"Your fancy car takes fancy parts, quite expensive, too," Mick added. "But you feel free to keep ol' Gertie until your car is done."

"Gertie?"

"The truck," Mick clarified with a chuckle. "She's not the prettiest, but you won't find a more dependable mode of transportation. How long you in town for anyway?"

Too damn long.

"I'll be here through the holidays. But, I can give…uh, Gertie back. I'm sure someone else will need it."

"Oh, no. Nothing but the best for William's grandson," Mick stated. "We sure do miss him around here. He'd stop in once a week with homemade brownies. Your grandmother started that and after she passed, he kept up the tradition. There's nothing like Erma Jackson's brownie recipe."

Nostalgia hit him once again. The flash of sitting on the porch swing with his grandpa when his gram would bring out a plate of warm brownies hit him hard. He'd forgotten all about that time. One summer ran into another in his mind and he didn't recall a memory without that front porch swing involved. Many conversations were had, some life decisions were made but mostly he and his grandpa would talk about nothing…which meant everything.

"Thanks for the call," Brady said, circling back to the reason Mick contacted him. "Just let me know when my car is ready."

He disconnected the call, and a little twinge of guilt burst through him at the abrupt ending, but he really didn't want to travel down memory lane with anyone. Going down that road alone was hell enough.

Brady blew out a sigh as he placed his phone on the counter and focused back on the unexpected delivery from Mad Batter. Considering his mood wasn't the best, he opted to say nothing right now. He'd call Violet later and thank her.

He wished like hell she wasn't so nice, that she didn't have a long-standing relationship with his grandfather. She'd be much easier to say no to and possibly ignore.

But she was wearing him down. He could feel it. This whole town was wearing him down and he hadn't even been here a full week yet. What the hell would two months do to him?

Everyone knew his grandparents, everyone wanted to talk about them. They talked to Brady as if they knew him personally, too. He was an outsider only passing through.

The chime at the end of the drive indicating a visitor echoed through the first floor. Now what? He didn't have time for visitors or gifts or anything else. Didn't people know he just wanted to be left alone to go through all of his grandfather's things, figure out what to do with all this stuff, and quietly slip back to Atlanta where he would hopefully still have a position at the law firm.

No doubt the unwanted visitor was Miss Calhoun, likely coming to check that her box of goodies made it on time. She was smart, he'd give her that. She would likely come ply him with more Southern charm and megawatt smiles in an attempt to get her way.

While Brady wasn't in the mood for company, he also couldn't deny something about that woman intrigued him and, since he was being honest with himself, she turned him on.

When did a quirky lady who couldn't take no for an answer get his mind rolling into overdrive like this? He shouldn't think about her, shouldn't think how sexy she looked in that stupid Halloween costume…but those red heels. He was a sucker for red and heels.

Raking a hand over the back of his neck, Brady made his way through the foyer to the front door. As he stepped out onto the porch, he didn't recognize the car pulling into the circular drive in front of the house.

He ignored that sliver of disappointment realizing that Violet wasn't his mystery guest. Just as well. The more detached from her he could stay, the better. And the more time that lapsed between visits would be one step closer to him getting out of here and back to Atlanta.

Brady stood at the threshold and watched as an elderly

woman stepped from her car. Her frail hand came to the top of her doorframe as if to steady her. Brady crossed the porch and headed down the steps. He didn't know who she was, but he couldn't just stand there and do nothing.

As he rounded the back of the car, the lady glanced up and gasped.

"Oh, I didn't see you there." She reached for the handle of the back door and pulled something from the seat. "I was hoping I'd catch you home. I made you some beef and noodles."

Out came an old yellow crockpot and Brady quickly took the dish from her. She offered a smile and he tried like hell to recognize who she was. Clearly she knew him.

Her silver hair had been styled up in a tight bun, her makeup minimal, but the pink lipstick stood out. She had diamond earrings, a cardigan and dress pants, and looked like she could've been a former librarian or a Sunday school teacher. Still, he wasn't sure who she was.

"I'm sorry I can't stay and visit," she told him. "I'm on my way to my Bible study class. I just wanted to bring you something to eat and welcome you back to town. It's been a long time since you visited."

That voice. He knew it.

Her eyes narrowed, but she smiled. "Don't tell me you don't remember your old kindergarten teacher, young man."

Brady laughed, recognition settling in. "No, ma'am. I wouldn't tell you that."

She scoffed. "At least you're still a gentleman. Your grandfather would be proud of you for coming back and taking over the family home."

Brady opened his mouth to correct her, but she patted his cheek.

"It's so good to see you, Brady. I need to get going, but I'll be back for a visit when I can stay longer. I can get my crockpot then. Enjoy those noodles. I remember that was your favorite dish at one time. Your grandmother always made sure to have them ready when your father would drop you off for your summer visits."

Was nothing ever forgotten in this town? People not only knew your business, they spoke about it so freely.

"I do love them," he admitted, though he hadn't had the dish for years. Probably since he visited here last. "I appreciate it."

Mrs. Baker smiled and nodded as she eased back into her driver's seat. Brady steadied the crockpot with one arm and closed her door with the other.

"You're welcome back anytime," he told her, realizing he meant it and this was the first person he wasn't surly with.

Once Mrs. Baker was gone, Brady took the homemade dish inside and realized he hadn't eaten much that day. He'd gotten up early and gone for a run, then he'd come home and made an omelet. That had been hours ago.

He set the crockpot on the kitchen counter and plugged it in. Though it was still warm, he wanted to keep it good and hot. He didn't recall the last time he had a real home-cooked meal. Eggs or a protein drink didn't count.

Brady made his way back through the hallway to the study on the first floor on the opposite side of the house. The moment he hit the threshold, he stopped short.

This entire room was a complete disaster. All he could do was stare at the mess he'd created. He wished like hell this task didn't fall to him, but his father was off with his younger, newer wife, traveling the globe, and couldn't be bothered with such things. Perhaps that's why William had left the estate to Brady.

But there was so much pressure to be the one to decide what should stay and what should go…likely William was hopeful that Brady would want to live here, but that just wasn't the lifestyle for him.

Brady's eyes roamed around the room as he took a step in.

What the hell did he do with all of these pictures? His grandmother had been a sucker for the camera, wanting every memory documented. Once she passed, the camera practically got cobwebs on it. But there were decades of photographs to go through and honestly, Brady didn't want to throw any away. Where would he store all of those? His condo in Atlanta couldn't house them and he didn't have siblings to share them with.

So now he would have to really narrow things down or try to get a storage facility to house things he couldn't part with.

The longer he stood here, the more he realized he was only getting more questions than answers. So many choices and suddenly those two months that seemed like forever, now seemed such a short time to condense years' worth of his family's life.

The deafening silence grated on his nerves. The tick-tick-tick of the grandfather clock from the foyer seemed to echo down the hallway.

How had his grandfather lived like this? The house seemed even larger with only one person in it. Brady refused to let himself get swept away in the recollections of each summer cookout with the yard and patio filled with family and friends, all of those cheery Christmas parties, the past tours and the people parading through the home.

Each room told a story…he just didn't know if he'd ever be ready to listen.

At least where his condo was in Atlanta, he had city noise and he could always just go down and grab a coffee or a drink at the local shops. He never felt alone there.

The chime at the end of the drive sounded once again and Brady was tempted to ignore it. After a short mental battle with himself, he made his way to the front of the house and spotted Violet's Jeep coming to a stop.

Why did just the sight of her produce a whole cocktail of emotions? Annoyance? Well, sure, because she was so damn relentless. But, there was a heavy dose of attraction he couldn't explain and an intrigue he didn't want to delve into.

Brady kept coming to the same conclusion, though. His willpower was slipping here and if he didn't watch out, he'd lose sight of the life he desperately wanted to get back to.

Chapter Seven

*It's time to switch from regular anxiety to fancy
Christmas anxiety.*
* Violet Calhoun

With care and purpose, Violet eased the large wreath
from the back of her Jeep. She bumped the half door with
her hip to close it and turned toward the wide porch. Her
breath caught in her throat at the sight of Brady standing between two of the entry columns, his hands on his
hips, staring down at her.

Mercy, that man could make a woman forget her purpose, but she was on a mission and it wasn't to get sidetracked by the sexy man glaring back at her.

And since when did he wear glasses? Because that
whole wide-shoulder sexy vibe combined with the studi-
ous vibe was more than even she could handle. He wore
another pair of dark dress pants and a light blue dress
shirt with the sleeves folded up on his forearms.

"Good evening," she sang in her most chipper tone.
She knew how that would aggravate him, but she couldn't
help herself. "I hope I didn't interrupt anything."

"Would you care if you did?" he asked as she started
up the steps.

Violet gasped. "Brady, despite what you think, I'm really not out to annoy you."

He muttered something beneath his breath, but she couldn't understand him. Probably best that she didn't know his true thoughts. Hearing his grumblings out loud was more than enough.

However, she could fight with the best of them and Brady had no clue what he was up against.

"I wanted to drop off a little peace offering," she told him, holding up the wreath. "I know just the perfect spot to hang it if you don't mind."

Brady stared at her for another minute, then crossed his arms over his broad chest. She'd made it two steps down from him and he still seemed like lord of his castle…or the dragon keeping her out, she couldn't tell.

"Do you have a hammer and a nail?" she asked as she offered a smile.

With a shake of his head, Brady stepped back and allowed her onto the porch. Violet took that gesture as a green light to head on inside the open door. A piece of her heart cracked at the emptiness. No hat hanging on the hall tree, the pictures had been taken off the walls, and a quick glance into the living area also showed a bare mantel.

He was seriously clearing things out and even though she didn't have much of an emotional tie to the house, she didn't like this swift change.

"You're really digging right into this moving on and getting out of here, aren't you?" she asked when Brady stepped inside. "What are you doing with all of William's things?"

He shrugged and closed the door at his back. "Right now I'm putting stuff in the study and then I'll prioritize them. Knickknacks and pictures are the biggest thing I need to go through. The furniture doesn't have any sentimental value to me so I can sell the house with all furnishings."

Ugh. Back with that again. Couldn't he focus on something more positive and cheerful? Did anything make this guy smile or even laugh? And for pity's sake, did he own casual clothes?

Violet glanced from the living room to Brady. "I didn't think anything held a sentimental value with you."

Something flashed through his eyes, but was gone before she could attempt to identify the emotion. Well, at least he had some reaction. She was starting to think he was void of feelings.

"Just because I'm selling this house doesn't mean I'm cold inside," he told her. "I just have a life of my own and it doesn't happen to be here."

She honestly didn't care where he lived or whenever he decided to go back, so long as he ultimately agreed with her perfect plan.

"Well," she sighed, turning her attention toward the front living area. "Since you already have this space cleaned out, I'll just set this right here. I won't even need that hammer and nail. Sometimes the casual look is best."

She propped the large wreath on the mantel, really wishing she'd known about the blank space. A white lantern or some tall, fat candlesticks would have gone a long way. Oh, maybe some garland and a couple stockings to really pull the nostalgia from the past.

Her mind set into overdrive for this fireplace. There was nothing more Christmasy than a well-decorated fireplace. She continued to arrange the branches and the ribbon just right since everything had shifted in the commute.

Violet stepped back and admired her work, little work that it was, and turned to face Brady. Nothing about decorating or events ever felt like work. She lived for each day she could wake up and do over again what she so loved.

"I had thought about hanging it on the landing right at the top, but this space really needs brightened up."

Brady leaned against the doorframe and stared toward the wreath. "It looks nice."

Violet couldn't help but laugh. "Well, a compliment. I'll take it, though I do believe that my creations are a little bit better than nice."

His gaze darted back to her. "You made that?"

"Who else? Of course I made that. It's what I do."

"I thought you were an events coordinator."

"I can't count the number of hats I wear," she told him. "Events Coordinator is just a nice way to sum up the fact I make things happen and in the end they look damn good."

His lips quirked and she cursed herself for getting a kick of arousal at his mouth.

"Sounds like you should change your slogan," he replied.

"I already have too many business cards printed," she volleyed back. "So, what about a Christmas tree? Something in the entryway with the high ceilings?"

"No tree."

"Even the Grinch had a tree," she told him.

The muscle ticked in his jaw and he removed his glasses as he held her gaze. "The Grinch stole a tree, there's a difference."

"Semantics." She waved a hand and laughed. "I can bring you one and you won't have to lift a finger."

"I'd hate to put you out. I'll be just fine with the wreath."

On a sigh, Violet turned and took in the cozy living area with high ceilings and classy furnishings. Dark woods, white upholsteries, original crown moldings... this place just begged to be decorated. He was going to be a tough man to battle with, but she rather enjoyed their little banter. It wasn't often she was faced with a challenge and one so sexy at that.

"I can practically hear your mind working."

She tossed a glance over her shoulder. "It never shuts off. I even dream about work."

Brady flashed a hint of a smile and if she thought he was attractive while being surly, that was nothing compared to the sexy grin.

"I'm assuming that's something we have in common," she commented when he remained silent.

"I'm an attorney," he reminded her. "My mind is always working."

She bet he was a total badass in the courtroom and she wouldn't mind seeing him in action. All suited up with that low voice and commanding presence.

Down, girl. Focus.

"Well, as much as I'd love to stay and discuss all the ways we are alike, I need to get home to my frozen dinner."

"Stay."

Violet stilled, shocked at the simple word that came out of his mouth. From the wide-eyed look on his face, Brady was just as stunned at his command.

"My kindergarten teacher just stopped by and delivered beef and noodles," he went on, swiping a hand down his face, for the first time showing nerves. "There's enough in there to feed ten people."

"Homemade beef and noodles? That has to be from Mrs. Baker," Violet guessed. "She loves to cook for people."

"She just left so they're still warm."

Violet pursed her lips and shrugged. "I could be persuaded to stay."

No way was she going to admit she wanted to stay to talk to him, to look at him, to figure out what the hell had her so intrigued with him.

Violet realized in that second that she wanted to stay not because of the tour, but because she was a woman with an attraction she hadn't felt in so long, she'd be a fool to ignore it.

Then again, she might be a bigger fool for staying.

Brady had no clue what the hell he was doing. He hadn't even thought of asking her to stay until the word slipped out. At that point, he couldn't exactly retract the invitation without sounding like a jerk.

So here they sat at the kitchen island on bar stools sharing a meal and he had nobody to blame but himself. But, if he was being honest, she intrigued him. She pushed him out of his comfort zone and something about her, other than being somewhat annoying and pushy, was refreshing. She wasn't like other women he knew. She was strong, independent, and quirky. Not qualities that usually went together, but damn it, she stirred something in him.

"How much willpower did it take for you to only bring

one Christmas item here?" he asked as he took a drink of his sweet tea.

Violet laughed and Brady stilled. That soft noise seemed to envelop him, wrapping him in a warmth he hadn't experienced for a long time. Every minute he spent with her he found himself drawn more and more into her web.

"I don't think I've ever just put up one decoration at a time anywhere," she admitted. "If you're looking for more, I do have some totes in my car with candlesticks and garland."

Brady found himself smiling. "I think we'll just stick with the wreath."

Violet shrugged and dug into her beef and noodles. "Suit yourself, but I'm going to wear you down."

Yeah, that's what he was afraid of…and not just with the decorations.

"So, do you have a family back in Atlanta?" she asked, scooping up another hearty bite.

Brady quirked his brow. "Is that a way of asking me if I'm single?"

Her eyes darted up to his. "Just making conversation. I mean, you're not that bad to look at, but I was curious."

Not that bad to look at? Brady straightened his back and squared his shoulders. Was that a compliment? "Don't hold back."

"I typically don't." She set her fork down and offered a smile. "I have a feeling your ego gets enough of a boost and you don't need more from me. You've seen yourself in the mirror. You know what you look like."

Damn it if she didn't amuse him, and he couldn't help but enjoy himself. "What do I look like?" he asked.

Violet rolled her eyes and took a drink of her tea. "All

dark and surly. A little wounded, if I was guessing, but definitely all business all the time. You make an intriguing package."

Interesting what she saw and a little too discomforting that she caught that wounded vibe just from his physical appearance. Maybe he wasn't getting enough sleep. Perhaps he should work on that a little more, but when he lay in bed in the dark of night, his mind kept working in overdrive and he couldn't get away from himself. Quiet was definitely the enemy when dealing with guilt and grief.

"I wouldn't exactly call myself surly," he muttered as he went back to his meal.

"Oh, you are. Trust me."

He had nothing else to say to that comment, so he finished his dinner and once they were both done, he set their dishes in the sink.

"I'll wash those," she told him as she came around the island.

"I'll get them later. Not a big deal."

He didn't know what to do with her now unless he wanted to talk about the sale of the home, which was shaky ground. All of this was uncharted territory for him: the house, the intimate dinner, the woman who was virtually a stranger.

"I can head on out," she told him. "Thanks for the dinner. That was much better than the Pizza Pocket I was going to pop into the microwave."

Brady wrinkled his nose. "That sounds disgusting."

"It's not the greatest." She crossed her arms and leaned against the island. "What do you have for dinner on a typical night back in Atlanta? Wait, let me guess. I bet you meet up with some buddies at an upscale pub to unwind with a craft beer and wings, that is if you're not impressing ladies at a posh restaurant, where you'll order an expensive bourbon."

She didn't know how far from the truth she was. But he'd let her play her little game because knowing that she'd actually put some thought into his personal life turned him on even more for reasons he didn't want to explain, even to himself.

"What about you?" he asked, dodging her question. "Do you always go for junk for dinner?"

"Honestly, the cooking gene skipped me. My mother is an okay cook, not the best, but that was just something I was never really any good at. But I can make a mean place setting for any type of event in record time with very little effort."

"And mantels," he reminded her.

Her smile spread across her face. "You should see what I can do with a stairway."

The silence settled between them, but he didn't have that awkward, hurried feeling to get her out of here. Having someone to talk to actually felt…well, nice. Being here alone every evening had gotten so monotonous and draining.

"Follow me," he told her.

Her eyes widened. "Where?"

He motioned as he headed toward the back stairs off the kitchen. "Just come on."

Brady mounted the narrow, curved steps that used to be the servants' stairs when the home was built. He'd loved playing hide-and-seek here when he was little. His grandmother would be cooking homemade biscuits and gravy for breakfast and he'd sneak down and scare her from his room. Looking back, he realized she'd probably known when he was there, but she'd always pretended to be scared.

Brady led Violet down the hallway, but turned when he didn't hear her footsteps anymore.

"I've never been up here," she told him, her head practically on a swivel, checking out her new surroundings.

"Never?" he asked, turning to face her. "All those visits with my grandfather or the years of doing the tour?"

She peeked into one bedroom, but remained in the doorway. "The tours only stay on the main floors and there was no reason for me to come up here when visiting. This wide hallway and all of these large oak doors are incredible. I'd never leave this house if I lived here."

Brady couldn't deny the beauty of the home, but he was very much eager to leave and get back to his life, his career…if he could salvage it.

"Do you want the grand tour?" he asked.

She peered over her shoulder and smiled. Was she always so bubbly and happy? He didn't understand people like that.

"Go ahead and show me what you wanted, then we can do the tour."

She fell into step behind him and he led her to the study. He stopped in the doorway and gestured.

"This is what I'm dealing with." Brady couldn't believe he was showing anybody this mess, but he trusted Violet. "Since you're so good at organizing, care to offer advice?"

Violet gasped and he nodded in agreement. There was a ton of boxes, papers, pictures, knickknacks spread all over the room. And that wasn't all of the things hidden around the house. Every cubby and cabinet held family treasures and he knew two months here wouldn't be near enough to sort through all of this himself.

He wondered why he'd ever let Violet into this personal space, but on the opposite side of the spectrum, Brady found that he didn't quite want to let her go.

Chapter Eight

Keep your holiday diet balanced...
a cookie in each hand.
* Violet Calhoun

"It's overwhelming, I know."

Violet didn't take her eyes off the chaos of the room. "I agree there's quite a bit in here, but I just want to dive in and see what all I find. Family history is my favorite thing to uncover."

She stepped in carefully, not quite knowing where to go first. She stopped at a box with the flaps open and peered in. Photos in frames were stacked and she pulled out the first one.

The black-and-white image appeared to be from the forties and obviously the wedding day of Brady's grandparents. The simplicity of that time with the bride's knee-length white dress, her tiny bundle of flowers, a fascinator clipped to the side of her short, curly hair, and the dark suit of his grandfather really resonated something within Violet. Such a sweet picture capturing a memory that would live on forever.

Events weren't so blown up during that era, quite different from today's times. People didn't go overboard making each holiday or party the talk of the town. What people talked about was the love people had for each other and how long marriages lasted and families and babies.

Violet's vision blurred as she stared at the photo.

"Violet?"

Brady's tone pulled her back to the moment and she glanced over her shoulder. "This picture is beautiful."

He took a step closer, his eyes studying her. "Are you okay?"

Violet sniffed and smiled. "Oh, yes. Don't mind me. Just a little sentimental. My parents divorced when I was a teen and my mother is getting remarried next month. I just have a crazy amount of emotions bottled up in me."

"Divorce can be tough."

Violet carefully set the picture back in the box. "The divorce was difficult at first, but my parents have always remained friends. They just realized they weren't in love with each other anymore. My mother and my father's current wife are actually very good friends."

Brady's brows drew in. "That's not normal. I'm a divorce lawyer, I know what I'm talking about."

Violet couldn't help but laugh. Maybe that was what made him so grouchy and cynical. Did a good day at work even exist in that line of work?

"Yeah, well, we aren't a normal family," she told him. "I'm thrilled my mother is getting remarried to Porter. He's a great guy and they are so adorable together."

"Wait. Porter Crosby? The mayor?"

Violet nodded.

"He and my grandfather were really close."

"Yes, I know," Violet told him. "Sometimes we would

all three meet and discuss the upcoming tour just to make sure we were all on the same page for that year."

Maybe this was just another in she needed to get Brady to agree to the tour. She didn't want to hassle him. She'd have to ease her way into this, but time was not on her side.

"So, tell me what you want to happen in here." She shifted her attention back to the room. "Are you planning on keeping the photos and selling the décor? Or maybe stage the house with the décor and sell the house as move-in ready?"

His eyes seemed to travel around the room and she could practically see the battle waging within him. This had to be difficult. Maybe that's why he didn't want to be here. Maybe the memories and the loss were just too much for one person to bear. He'd needed a target to cling to and she just so happened to be in the right place at the right time. Violet always believed everything happened for a reason.

"Honestly, I have no clue. I feel guilty throwing anything out, but at the same time, I can't exactly keep it all."

Considering she'd never had to go through a loved one's things, Violet couldn't quite grasp the emotions he must be feeling. This wasn't her family and she hated the thought of any of these items going. How could anyone just box up someone's life? How did anyone decide what was important or what to let go of?

"If this were me, I would start one box at a time," she recommended. "Do you have cousins or aunts or uncles who would want anything? What about your father?"

Brady blew out a sigh. "My father and grandfather never made amends with their relationship before Grand-dad passed. I've tried calling Dad, but he's not returned my calls. He's off doing who knows what with his much younger wife. Another thing I see all too often with my clients."

Violet knew only a little about Brady's parents. Just what she'd picked up from William over the years, and she hadn't pried or questioned when he'd made comments. Brady's dad left his mom during some midlife crises and had been traveling all over the globe with his girlfriend. Apparently he was still sowing those proverbial wild oats, but was newly married now.

"This has to be doubly difficult for you," Violet told him, taking a step toward him.

She quickly realized she was within reaching distance and she pulled up every bit of her willpower to keep her hands to herself.

On one hand, she wanted to comfort him. Had anyone done that during this entire process? Who did he actually have to turn to? Perhaps that's why he was so disgruntled and irritable. He was dealing with so many emotions and he had no outlet and no shoulder to lean on.

There was so much more to Brady and his mind than what she'd first thought. She'd been so preoccupied with her own worries, she didn't take the time to consider his current state.

Second, there was something about that tough exterior of his that made her want to penetrate it and get inside where she suspected he was soft and vulnerable.

The attraction continued to pull at her and she seriously needed her common sense to prevail because neither one of them were in a position to pursue anything… that is, if he even felt this spark. Perhaps the tension was one-sided.

"Do you have time to stay?" he asked, his eyes drifting back to her.

"Stay?"

Brady nodded. A flash of that vulnerability came and went. "To help me make sense of some of this. You were close with my grandfather. Honestly, you saw him more in the past few years than I did."

Violet could go home and work on her mother's wedding or tighten more details for the tour, especially since *Simply Southern* would be here in a few short days.

But Brady wouldn't have asked if he didn't want her to stay. Maybe he had guilt for having to get rid of things or maybe he just didn't want to be alone with all the memories. Either way, Violet couldn't just leave.

She pulled in a deep breath and glanced around the room. "Where do you want to start?"

He gestured toward the boxes. "Start anywhere. I'll follow your lead."

Violet made her way around the room, stepping over and around various boxes and totes. She went to the wall of books and glanced over the spines and titles.

"This might be a good place," she told him. "There are so many books here. Are you going to try to keep them all?"

Brady came over to stand beside her. "I wouldn't have the space in my condo."

"Great. We can call the local library and have them donated. I'm sure William would have liked that."

Violet's cell in her pocket chimed and she pulled it out to see her mother's name light up the screen.

"Excuse me one minute," she told Brady.

Violet swiped the screen to answer.

"Hey, Mom."

"Honey, I hope I'm not interrupting."

"Not at all. What's up?"

"I was hoping we could go dress shopping Friday afternoon," her mother said. "I didn't know if that was an option for you? You know I'd love to have you and the girls all there. Can you check with them and see if they can make it? We'll do dinner after. My treat."

Violet's schedule ran through her mind and she figured she better go dress shopping before the media crew arrived in town. Her mother's wedding still took precedence over anything else.

"I'll talk to them, but I'm sure we can all make it," she assured her. "I'll text them now and let you know."

"Thank you, sweetheart. I'm so excited to have you by my side."

Violet smiled. "I wouldn't be anywhere else."

Once she disconnected the call, she shot off a text to Robin and Simone about the shopping trip. Vi slid the cell back into her pocket and turned back to Brady. Those dark eyes seemed so set on her, she couldn't help the jolt of awareness that shot through her.

"You don't need to stay," he told her after a moment. "I can sort this stuff."

"Oh, I'm fine. Just planning my mother's wedding. Between that, the tour, the magazine, there's always something going on."

He cocked his head to the side as if contemplating his words. "What do you do for fun?"

Confused, Violet shrugged. "I don't know. Decorate and plan, I guess. Why?"

"That's your job," he corrected. "I'm talking about fun."

"My job can't be fun?"

Brady's brows drew in and he eased himself onto the back of a sofa and seemed to be mulling over her question.

"I love what I do," she went on. "If you're in a career that you love, then it never feels like work."

"I don't think I've ever met someone like you," he muttered. "Work and fun are totally separate things."

"Says someone who lets his work rule his life."

"Work is my life," he countered.

"Well, I can't imagine anything is fun about helping people divorce."

"I don't cause the divorce. I just make sure my clients get what is due to them."

That sounded like a nightmare and so utterly lonely.

Violet knew there were people who hated their jobs, who let their careers run their lives, or whose only relationship was with their office and computer. She never wanted to feel that way. The minute her work stopped being fun and a blessing was the day she quit and found something else.

"You know you only have one life, right?" she asked.

He continued looking at her like she had three heads. Wow. This guy truly was oblivious to the joys he could be experiencing each day, the happiness surrounding him if he'd just open his eyes and see.

"What do you do for fun?" she tossed back at him.

Brady pursed his lips and finally shrugged. "Nothing you would relate to."

Intrigued, Violet took a seat on a stack of boxes and crossed her arms. "Try me."

He muttered something beneath his breath and she eased forward. "Excuse me?"

"Stars," he stated. "I like studying astronomy and the stars."

A dreamer. She never would've guessed. Granted if she called him out with that title, he wouldn't agree. He'd find some philosophical way to explain his hobby.

"And why do you think I wouldn't understand that?" she asked. "Astronomy sounds fascinating."

"I volunteer at a planetarium close to my condo on Saturday afternoons." Brady laughed. "I don't even know why I told you that. I haven't told anybody."

Why did he feel the need to remain so closed off? The more she uncovered about Brady Jackson, the more she wanted to know. The allure continued to grow and she wasn't even trying to fight it anymore. Why should she? What was one more thing on her plate?

"I've been told I'm a good listener," she replied. "Besides, I have nobody to tell so your secret is definitely safe with me. And I think it's great that you volunteer your time. Sounds like you do have something you love besides work."

She was impressed with what he'd revealed and she had no doubt that he never wanted her to know that much about his personal life.

"I can't believe you haven't brought up the tour," he told her. "Or are you plotting how to trick me into agreeing?"

She couldn't help but smile as she came to her feet. She plucked the lid off the box she'd been using as a seat and surveyed the contents.

"Oh, I'm always plotting," she assured him. "If you want to discuss the tour, I'm down for that."

When he remained silent, she picked up the envelope inside the box. There were multiple envelopes stacked neatly with no writing on the front. They had all already been opened, so she slid out the folded paper and smoothed out the creases.

The moment she started to read, she knew this was personal and something she shouldn't be looking at.

Violet quickly put the letter back in the envelope and neatly back into the box. After replacing the lid, she turned to Brady.

"What was it?" he asked, taking a step closer.

"I'm pretty sure it's a box of love letters."

"Love letters? To whom?"

"The one I saw was from your grandfather to your grandmother."

Brady stepped around her and lifted the lid back off the box. "There's a ton in here."

He looked at the box beneath that one only to find more envelopes similar to the first box.

"I wonder how many of these I'll find," he muttered.

"I'll leave that to you," Violet told him. "That's not something for me. I'll get in touch with the library about the books and how about I contact an antiques dealer to come give you a price for some of the knickknacks and décor you want off your hands?"

His eyes shifted from the box to her and the air around her seemed to crackle. She'd heard that term before, but never understood it before now.

The sun had almost set, with a very soft orange glow beaming through the windows. She'd stayed later than she thought, and while this certainly wasn't a date, she hadn't spent this much time alone with a man in a long time. Maybe she should make more time for her social life.

Once the holidays were over, of course. Granted, at

that time Brady would be gone. Funny how that realization dropped a sense of sadness within her. This man most definitely was not the one she should start getting attached to. Nothing good would ever come from hanging feelings on a temporary man.

"That would be great," he finally told her. "Just starting somewhere makes me feel like I'm making progress."

"Have you given any more thought to my proposition?"

His brow quirked and a corner of his mouth kicked up into a grin. Well, well, well. Maybe that attraction wasn't one-sided at all.

But, no. She had to keep this strictly business or, at the absolute most, just friendly. Not too friendly.

"The trade of the tour for me staging a grand open house party," she amended.

Brady nodded but remained close. Too close. Close enough to touch that dark stubble along his jaw, close enough to smell that woodsy scent she didn't expect from him, and close enough to realize his dark brown eyes had flecks of black that made him seem even sexier than she'd first thought.

And she'd thought quite a bit.

"The way you're looking at me doesn't seem like you want to talk business."

His low voice sent shivers through her. He leaned in just enough to close the final distance between them. Violet's heart seemed to beat faster than usual, her breath caught in her throat. She couldn't look away, couldn't step back. She wanted to know what he was going to do, what he wanted and if it was the same thing she wanted.

But what did she want? For him to kiss her? For him to slide his hands through her hair and take control?

Yes. That's exactly what she wanted.

"Maybe I wasn't thinking about the tour," she whispered, her eyes darting to his mouth.

"No?" He reached up and tucked her hair behind her ear, then trailed his fingertips along her jawbone. "What were you thinking when you were staring at me?"

He slid his other hand up and into her hair, tipping her head back just enough that she had to adjust to stare up at him. Her body fell against his and Violet would have to think about how hard and perfect that chest of his felt... later. Right now, she was worried he'd kiss her—and worried he wouldn't.

"Do you want me to kiss you, Vi?" he asked, his lips barely a whisper from hers.

Never one to play games or keep talking about what she wanted, she leaned up and covered his mouth with hers. The slight gasp that escaped him was a small victory in her favor. She imagined taking him off guard was quite unusual and that he always prided himself on control.

She also knew he hadn't set out to kiss her when he'd asked her to stay. But here they were and she was done analyzing it.

Violet slid her arms around his neck and opened for him. While she may have been wondering what kissing Brady would be like, nothing prepared her for the actual experience.

And this man was definitely an experience. The way he held her, the way he commanded her mouth and took control, something about that was so masculine and sexy.

He grazed his lips over hers before easing back. When he stared down at her without saying a word, Violet was tempted to dive back in, but she needed to control herself. Nothing was attractive about a woman throwing herself at a man.

"I should go."

Brady smiled. "I didn't take you for someone to run when things got awkward."

"I'm not awkward," she corrected. "I'm aroused and I'm leaving before we both cross a line we can't come back from."

Violet circled around him and let herself out before she revealed any more of her bold, blunt honesty. Though he should know where she stood. It wasn't like that kiss was cold. No, her entire body heated from one kiss while fully dressed with a man she should be persuading to see things her way…not see her as his lover.

Violet looked in her rearview mirror as she pulled out of his long drive. She had other homes to decorate and other preparations to make for the Tinsel Tour.

Unfortunately, all she could think of was how her lips still tingled and her body still hummed after that very brief, yet powerful encounter.

Now she just had one more thing to keep her up at night and it had nothing to do with work.

Chapter Nine

Dear Santa, just leave your credit card under my tree.
* Violet Calhoun

"Oh, Lori, that one is gorgeous."

Lori smoothed a hand down her dress and turned side to side in the three-way mirror. The knee-length blush pink dress showed off her petite frame, and from the smile on her face, she loved this one.

"You said that the last five dresses I tried on, Robin."

Violet leaned back on the plush white couch and crossed her legs. "That's because you've been gorgeous in all of them."

"It's true," Simone agreed. "You're not making this very easy for us."

Lori turned to face them and held her hands out to her sides. "Well, I do love this one," she said. "But is it worth the price? Why do I always go to the most expensive?"

"I'll buy it for you, Mom."

Her mother glanced to Vi. "I can afford it, I just don't know if I should splurge."

Violet came to her feet and laughed. "I'm well aware you can afford it, but I want to buy it. I want to do this for you and you look so stunning. Your smile was different when you came out, so I think you feel this is the one."

She blew out a sigh and turned back to the mirror. "I really do."

"It's such a beautiful shade on you," Robin stated. "A perfect neutral for any colors of flowers you want. We can do classic with whites and gold accents, that would still tie into Christmas."

Lori's eyes met Violet's in the mirror. "Is this the wrong color for a Christmas wedding?"

"Since when do you care about being traditional?" Violet asked. "It's your wedding so you can do whatever you like. There are no rules."

"Then this is the one I want," Lori said with a wide grin on her face.

Violet stepped up onto the round platform and wrapped her arms around her mother. Their eyes continued to hold each other's.

"I'm so excited for you," Violet told her. "I've never seen you so happy. Porter is one lucky man."

Before Violet could say anything else, her cell rang from her purse.

"Sorry, I need to grab this." She stepped off the platform and reached for her bag. "You guys go ahead and start with accessories. I'll be right along."

"We'll wait," Simone stated. "No rush."

Violet pulled out her cell and stilled when she saw Brady's name on the screen. She hadn't spoken to him since the incident…the one that still left her with all sorts of arousing fantasies and thoughts.

She cleared her throat and answered. "Brady."

"I hope this isn't a bad time."

That low, throaty tone of his sent even more shivers

through her than she wanted to allow, but she had zero control where he was concerned. He'd been somewhat accurate when he'd told her she was running. She'd had to. Otherwise she would've ended up trying to strip him down to see if he was as muscular as he felt.

Violet glanced up, noticing all eyes were on her. She offered a smile to her friends and her mom before turning her back on them once more.

"This is fine. What's up?"

"I'm not sure when you were expecting the people from the magazine, but they just showed up at my house."

Violet nearly choked on her breath. "What?"

"I take that to mean you didn't send Lauren and Bryce here."

"Hell no I didn't send anyone there," she cried. Violet grabbed her purse and motioned for everyone else to get going. "I'll call you back. No, I'll come by. No, wait. I don't know what I'll do yet, but I'll be in touch."

She disconnected the call and tried not to panic, but that was like telling her not to breathe. This wasn't how things were supposed to work out. Each part of her life and the days to come had been organized in a timely manner and she had to keep that outline or everything would fall apart…like her sanity.

"What is wrong?" her mother asked, stepping down to stand by Violet.

"The magazine folks are here," she told them. "That was Brady. He said they stopped by his house. They weren't supposed to be here until Monday. They're too early. How in the world do I handle this? Everything has a date and a time. Showing up three days early is not part of my plan."

Violet shoved her cell in her purse and pulled her hair

back from her face. "Brady thought I sent them to his house," she went on. "I thought he was calling to discuss the kiss, but no, he called to accuse me of—"

"Wait." Simone held up her hand. "Calm down, stop the nervous chatter, and forget the magazine folks. What the hell is this about a kiss?"

Violet gripped her purse strap on her shoulder and stared at her friends and her mother. None of them seemed to be in the same panic and Violet hadn't even realized she'd let anything slip out about the kiss.

That's what happened when her mouth started working faster than her common sense. Damn it, how did she backpedal out of this one? She didn't have time to explain, she had visitors to go greet.

"You kissed Brady?" Robin asked, her eyes wide and unblinking. "And said nothing to us?"

"Why is this just now coming out?" her mother asked. "How long ago did you kiss? We're going to need wine for this."

Violet rubbed her head, already feeling the onslaught of a headache. Why didn't she just grab her stuff and go? They would have understood her urgency. But, no. She had to run her mouth and now her crew was waiting on an answer she wasn't ready to give.

"Can we talk about this later?" she demanded. "There's a journalist and a photographer in town who I really should go greet and figure out what all is going on and if they need anything from me since I wasn't planning on them for another three days."

Her mother pursed her lips. "Considering you're stressed and I'm adding to it, I'll let you off the hook... for now. But we will revisit this conversation."

A bit of pressure eased off her shoulders until she

turned to her friends. Simone seemed to be staring daggers through her. Robin still seemed stunned.

"Listen," Violet started. "The very short story is we kissed and that's all. Nothing else happened, that wasn't supposed to happen, and it won't happen again. Okay? Are we good now? Because I really need to get going."

Without waiting for their reply, she kissed her mother on the cheek. "I'll leave my credit card with the associate and you can bring it to me later. Simone will give you a ride home. Stay and pick out anything you want to go with it."

"Wait a minute." Robin held up her hands. "Let me go. This is your mother's day and she'll want you here. I'll go and talk with them. How about that?"

Violet thought about it and realized that wasn't a terrible idea. "Are you sure?"

Robin nodded. "Positive. They want to speak to all of us anyway, so there's no reason I can't go introduce myself and get a feel for what they want."

Reaching out to hug her friend, Violet breathed a small sigh of relief. "That would be great. Why don't you go ahead and set up a breakfast meeting tomorrow and we can all meet up then?"

Robin nodded and reached for her purse. "Consider it done."

Once Robin was gone, Violet shifted her focus back to her mother.

"Okay. Let's find shoes and jewelry."

"Seriously?" Simone laughed. "You think we're just going to move on after you dropped that bomb about a kiss?"

Violet stared at her friend. She truly didn't want to

get involved with this now…or ever, but that was clearly impossible.

"The kiss was nothing," Violet insisted.

Lying had never been her strong suit, but she hoped she was at least a little believable. How could she answer any questions when she was still trying to process everything herself?

"It must have been something or you wouldn't have jumped to the conclusion that Brady would call you about it," her mother chimed in.

Always the voice of reason, that woman. Right now, though, Violet didn't want to get into this in the middle of the Brides and Belles Bridal Shop.

"How is everyone doing here?"

Violet turned to the sales associate and nearly kissed the woman for interrupting. When they'd arrived for the appointment, the associate had pulled several items and then left them alone, promising to be back to check on them later. Her timing was perfect.

"Oh, that dress was made for you," the lady claimed, all of her attention on Lori. "Don't move. I know the exact earrings and bracelet set that will look stunning on you."

She dashed off just as quick as she came and Violet found herself the center of attention once again. Damn. So much for a break.

"Listen, when I'm ready to talk, I will," she explained. "If there's anything to discuss, I promise to let you guys know. Got it? Now, can we focus on the wedding and not a kiss that meant nothing?"

Simone nodded. "Fine, but only because we're pressed for time and we all have so much going on. But don't forget, that man is married to his job. I don't want you hurt."

"Hurt?" Violet laughed. "Sims, it was a kiss. We're not dating."

"Not yet," Simone muttered just as the sales clerk strolled back in with accessories.

Violet hurried to help her mother and ooh and ahh in the mirror with the sales associate. The entire time Simone continued to make judgmental glances Violet's way. Vi merely smiled at the reflection of her friend.

Once everything was finalized and her mother looked ridiculously stunning, Violet went to the front desk and paid for everything. Her credit card was going to take a major hit these next few weeks. She didn't want to dip too much into the city's already stretched budget, but she did want to make sure everything was perfect for photo ops with the journalists.

"So, who has time to get some Christmas shopping in?" Lori asked as soon as they stepped outside the store.

The afternoon sun beat down, giving a nice warmth to the chill in the air. All of the streetlights had greenery spiraling up to the top with red berries mixed into the arrangement. Shops had large black pots outside of their storefronts. The pots overflowed with evergreen, poinsettias, and sprigs of white stems. The Garden Club had really outdone themselves with the way they had decorated Magnolia Lane.

"I'm done Christmas shopping," Violet told them. "And I need to check in on Robin."

"Why are you always done so damn early?" Simone complained. "You make the rest of us look bad."

Violet shrugged. "I like to shop for gifts all year. Don't worry, you'll love yours."

"Well, you're getting nothing from me until I get all the details about Brady."

Violet rolled her eyes and pulled her car keys from her bag. "Then save your money because I've already said it meant nothing. Now, I have to run."

Violet kissed her mother goodbye and waved to Simone. The sooner she could escape, the better. She had some greetings to make with the magazine folks and she had to talk to Brady. Time was up and he was going to have to let her into the house to decorate and she'd have to offer up *almost* anything to get him to agree.

Chapter Ten

Alexa, put up the rest of these decorations.
* Violet Calhoun

Brady thought for sure Violet would be on his doorstep as soon as they hung up. The woman continued to surprise and intrigue him.

He also thought she had sent those people to the house to start taking photos of the usual grand dame of the Tinsel Tour. When he'd accused her, she genuinely sounded surprised that they'd showed up. Obviously she'd been caught just as off guard.

Brady pulled in a deep breath and put his weights down. He'd ordered some basic gym equipment and set up an area in the master bedroom. He'd always tried to keep up his workout regime no matter how hectic his work schedule and court dates. There was something therapeutic about sweating and pushing your body to the best of its ability.

But even lifting an extra round of weights and pounding out a few more miles on the treadmill didn't help. Violet and that damn kiss had been rolling through his mind nearly every minute since it happened...and he quickly realized he wanted more. More kisses, more touches, just…more.

Brady swiped the sweat from his forehead with the back of his arm and reached for his water bottle. As he downed the drink, he checked his emails and texts. Nothing. Not a damn thing.

Okay. So he made a mistake with his outburst against another attorney outside the courtroom and he'd been told by the partners of the firm to take a breather before coming back. But Brady thought they'd at least check in or keep him in the loop. Everyone had a breaking point, right?

He'd heard absolutely nothing since leaving. Did that mean he wouldn't be welcome back? Did that mean he was out of the running to make the third partner? After all these years, all they had been through together, and all the hours Brady had poured into his career, everything could be gone and he'd have to start from scratch.

He didn't have much of an excuse for his behavior the past few months. When his grandfather died there was a stirring of emotions he didn't want to face…and still hadn't delved into. Then one case after another kept piling up and Brady tried to be all things to all people while dealing with his own pain and guilt.

There was no way he was going to let his dreams of being a partner in a law firm pass him by over a mistake he made. He could learn from his mistakes, and everyone deserved a second chance—didn't they?

Brady stripped his shirt and draped it over his shoulder as he headed toward the master bath for a quick shower. He'd grill a steak and enjoy a beer on the patio this evening and force himself to relax.

Actually, since coming here, he had somewhat relaxed.

Clearly there was nothing to do as far as work was concerned. Now his stress came from all of this stuff and the fiery sprite who loved Christmas more than life itself.

He was stunned she hadn't shown up with a twelve-foot-tall tree and a million white lights and who knew what else she probably traveled with in case of emergencies. Brady wondered if she ever gave up. Would she ever just move on with her efforts and put them to use someplace better?

Surely there were other people who lived for this Tinsel Tour. Right? Like, the entire town seemed to close down for the event if he recalled correctly. When Brady had been younger, he'd accompanied his grandfather to a couple of the tours. At the time, Brady didn't care much about the homes or the décor, but his grandfather was all over the annual event.

All Brady had cared about at the time were the cookies and treats set out at each home. One place always put out homemade cherry tarts and they were his absolute favorite.

Brady had just reached in to turn on his shower when the doorbell rang. Tempted to ignore it and continue about his evening, he figured whoever came to see him probably needed something.

There were few people who stopped by. It could be another blast from his past with more homemade meals, it could be the journalists again, or it could be Violet. He'd bank all his money on the latter.

Brady bounded down the steps and started tugging his shirt on as he opened the door. Sure enough, Violet stood on the other side. Her eyes immediately dropped to his abdomen a split second before he pulled his shirt lower.

"Uh...did I interrupt something?" she asked.

Brady took in her crazy candy cane leggings and off the shoulder red T-shirt and shook his head.

"Just getting ready to hit the shower," he told her. "Were you able to break out of Santa's workshop?"

"You're hilarious," she told him with that dry tone as she brushed past him and stepped inside. "I'm shocked you're out of your suits. I was beginning to wonder if you had real clothes."

"I wear dress shirts and dress pants," he countered. "Suits are for the courtroom and they are, indeed, real clothes."

She raised her brows like she wanted to argue, but replied, "I didn't come to argue, though we are so good at it. We need to talk about the theme for your house."

"Theme?" he asked.

She stood in the foyer with her arms crossed, looking as if he was putting her out with his confusion. This wasn't a game or just for fun. She confused the hell out of him on a regular basis.

"You know, for the tour," she added. "Every house has a theme. We have a Nutcracker House, a Little Drummer Boy House, the Mrs. Claus's Kitchen House. There are fifteen in all including yours."

Brady wanted to make her go away, but he honestly knew he was fighting a losing battle. With a sigh of defeat, he nodded.

"Fine," he said. "Do whatever you want. I don't care anymore."

"Really?" Her voice hitched up a notch and she clasped her hands together. "I don't have to beg or use my charms?"

"No begging, please. It's exhausting."

And that's likely how she wore down her prey.

"I promise, once this tour is over, I will stage this home and throw an open house extravaganza like you've never seen."

Brady took a step forward and rested his arm on the banister alongside where Violet stood. He liked the way her breath hitched and her eyes widened as he came closer. Something about knowing he had such an effect on her was even more intriguing and arousing.

"So this theme for the tour…what all does that entail?"

"I have something out here for you."

Just as she started past him, Brady reached and grabbed her arm. Her eyes went from his hold to his lips. Her warm breath fell on his face as they were so close…closer than he'd intended.

"You want to talk about it?" he asked.

Her eyes landed on his, then dropped back down. "Probably not a good idea."

No, it probably wasn't, but that didn't seem to mean a damn thing right now.

Brady closed the gap between them, slowly grazing his lips over hers to give her plenty of time to talk him out of this insanity. But she opened for him, offering herself, and Brady circled her waist with his hands, pulling her flush against his body.

Her hands went to his shoulders and those short nails of hers bit into his skin through his shirt. A soft moan slipped from her, and his entire body lit up from within. There was a passion in this woman he hadn't expected from her quirkiness.

The doorbell rang, jerking Brady from…hell, he didn't know what they were doing. But he didn't appreciate the interruption.

He glanced at the door, finding Violet's friend Simone standing there looking none too happy.

There was only one thing worse than an unwanted guest and that was an angry unwanted guest.

"Oh, no," Violet muttered, then quickly stepped back.

Well, nothing like being treated like a dirty little secret.

Ignoring that jab of pain he shouldn't feel, Brady went to the door and opened it.

"Sorry to interrupt your meeting," Simone said, her eyes only on Violet. "I went to see Robin thinking I'd catch you there, but she said you were coming here to talk to Brady about the theme for his house. If what I saw was any indication, we're going to need to put a PG-13 rating on the tour."

Violet stepped forward. "Don't be like that. It was just a kiss."

Again, he shouldn't be hurt by those words, but he was. And maybe it was *just a kiss*, but wasn't that something they should discuss in private?

"That's what you said about the other kiss," Simone stated. "Anyway, I'm not here to judge."

"Yet you're doing just that," Brady added, unable to keep his mouth shut.

Simone turned her attention to him. "I just need to talk to Violet, if you don't mind."

Brady shrugged and headed toward the back of the house. He might not have gotten that shower yet, but he could at least get his steak prepped for grilling.

He knew he wasn't Simone's favorite person. Their short-lived dating experience had turned them both off each other. Who knows what she was saying right now to Violet, but Brady was sure he didn't want to know. If

Simone knew he was back here seasoning a fat, juicy steak, she'd probably come stab him. The woman was a die-hard vegetarian…which was fine, but she didn't need to push her beliefs onto him.

Simone and Violet seemed like total opposites. Brady laughed as he flipped the steak and sprinkled the salty mixture onto the other side. Perhaps that difference in personalities was exactly why he was drawn to Violet. The kissing definitely didn't hurt, either.

Brady went up the back steps of the house toward his master suite. He didn't want to disrupt the girls in the foyer. He'd heard Simone's voice raise once and he was smart enough to steer clear of an angry woman.

He showered quickly and changed into another pair of gym shorts and a T-shirt before heading back downstairs via the kitchen stairs. Just as he hit the last step, he heard the front door close.

Brady made his way through the hallway and back into the foyer where Violet stood glancing down at her phone.

"Are you sticking around?" he asked.

Her head shot up, her eyes wide like she hadn't even heard him approach. "What? Oh, um…yeah. If you don't mind. We still need to discuss theme and times I can get a few of the volunteers here to decorate."

Brady nodded. "That's fine. Were you raked over the coals by your friend?"

Violet winced. "Only a little, but she means well. I get that you two didn't hit it off when you dated those few times."

"That's an understatement."

Violet offered a smile and laid her phone on the accent table by the door. "Well, I'm not dating you. I'm working with you and neither of us have time for anything else. Right?"

Why did that irk him when she said that? Like she was just blowing off what they'd shared? Granted they hadn't exactly pledged anything to each other, but...

No buts. She was right. He didn't have time for anything. There was plenty on his plate without getting caught up in a sexy woman with all the right curves and a mouth made for kissing.

"Right," he finally agreed. "I just started dinner, so join me while we talk."

"Another dinner?" she asked with a wide smile. "Maybe we are dating and just don't know it."

Yeah...that's precisely what he was afraid of.

Chapter Eleven

Establish dominance by putting glitter
in your Christmas cards.
* Violet Calhoun

"We did the nutcrackers at the end of the Sampsons' drive last year like guards. For the Spencers', let's have them flank the front door since their porch is so wide with a high ceiling."

Violet ordered her team at the Spencer home to get underway. The folks from the magazine were due here any minute. They wanted to get photos of the decorating process in full swing and Violet didn't want them at Brady's house until that one was completely finished. She had something truly special planned for that one this year.

The crew got to work and Violet made notes on her phone for the Chamberlain home tomorrow. She wanted it to be a snowy scene with sleds and she still was racking her brain on a clever theme name for that one.

Violet stepped from the side porch and made her way around the front of the house just as the media crew pulled up. Last night she'd tried to meet up with them when she'd gone to see Robin, but the two guests had already checked into their B and B for the evening.

With a deep breath, Violet pasted on a smile and went to introduce herself. She'd only been in contact with the head editor, so Violet really hadn't met either of them before, but she was told their names in advance.

She did hear from Simone that Robin and the photographer were butting heads already, which intrigued and amused Violet. Robin never got into a verbal tussle with anyone. She was literally a peacemaker.

"Welcome," Violet called out as she descended the steps of the home. "You must be Lauren and Bryce. I'm Violet."

The curvy blonde smiled and extended her hand. "It's a pleasure to meet you. This is such an exciting project and we're thrilled we were the ones chosen to cover it."

Violet shook her hand and then turned to the guy. "We are so glad to have you all here."

"I'll be taking shots from every angle at times, so just ignore me," Bryce told her with a wide grin. "Or if I'm in your way, let me know. I still want you guys to carry on with your plans, but we do want to capture the full essence of the tour from start to finish."

"I understand," Violet replied.

She couldn't help but stare at the tall, broad man with dark eyes and a shaved head. She hadn't known what to expect them to look like, but a striking journalist and a sexy photographer certainly hadn't crossed her mind. She wondered if they were a couple or just coworkers.

Good grief. A few kisses with Brady and the wedding bells looming for her mother had her with hearts in her eyes. She needed to focus, and for the first year ever in her history of working the Tinsel Tour, she was having a difficult time.

"Where would you guys like to start?" Violet asked.

"I've got some volunteers who will be setting up here if you want some shots. I can take you on a drive around the other homes on the tour if you want me to give you the lay of the land, so to speak."

"Your friend Robin did that for us last night," Lauren commented. "You have some gorgeous homes in this area. It's going to be difficult to narrow down just a few for the spread."

Violet nodded. "I can't help you there because I love all the homes, and the people in this town are really great."

"Do you always have volunteers who help you with the decorating?" Lauren asked, glancing behind Violet to the crew bustling around on the porch.

"I do," Vi told them. "There are very detailed guidelines for each home, and every one has a theme. I go over everything beforehand with the volunteers and I'm hands-on somewhere in each process. I also always do the final look through to make sure everything is perfect."

Lauren's smile widened. "I love the idea of themes. That's really fun. So, for now, maybe take us through this home and how you decide the different themes for each place."

Violet nodded and escorted the crew around the perimeter of the home, then she took them inside. The more she spoke about the process and how her ideas form, the more relaxed she became. This was her life, the thing she looked forward to the most.

As she spoke, she heard Bryce clicking with his camera behind her. She wondered what he would ultimately end up with and how this whole project would come out in the end.

"I would really love to get into the Jackson mansion,"

Lauren stated when they'd come back out front to their SUV. "We stopped by there, hoping to catch the owner, but it was a young guy and he said we'd have to talk to you."

"Did he?"

So he was putting the control in her corner. Good to know.

"Yes, the owner, William Jackson, was the one who started the Tinsel Tour fifty years ago." Violet pulled her sunglasses down to shield from the afternoon rays. "William passed away back in the summer, but I had been his right-hand woman for several years so the town council voted for me to take the reins now."

"From the looks of things, I'd say this town is in very good hands," Lauren told her. "We'd like to get some photos with you, Robin, and Simone at each of your businesses and then some of you together. Maybe in a central part of town or someplace that's meaningful to the citizens here."

"The park has a beautiful gazebo that's always decorated for the holidays," Violet informed her. "Many weddings are held there, so that would be one option."

"Sounds perfect." Lauren turned to Bryce. "Do you have all you need here?"

He nodded and eased his camera strap over his shoulder. "We're good."

"Great," Lauren said. "How about we plan on meeting tomorrow at your shop? I can do more of a personal interview about you and we can get some of those photos."

Violet nodded. "Sounds great. I open at ten. Would you like to come about nine?"

"We will be there."

After Lauren and Bryce left, Violet blew out a sigh

of relief. The initial meeting went really well, but she wondered how tomorrow would go. There wasn't much personal in her life that was exciting enough to warrant an interview.

She shot off a quick text to Robin and Simone telling them the game plan and to see when they could all three get together for the park session. She needed to talk to Brady and get a team there ASAP so they could get everything decorated. But the late start on his place would mean she'd have to pull people from other locations.

There was simply too much to do and they were running out of time to get everything done. Lauren and Bryce were supposed to be in town for the next ten days, which meant everything had to be done before they left so he could take all the appropriate photos.

As soon as they left town, Violet would be all hands on deck to pull off her mother's dream wedding day. As much as Vi didn't want to rush toward the holiday, preferring to enjoy each moment leading up to it, she also really wanted to get to that monumental day. She couldn't wait to see all of the hard work and plans come together for Porter and her mom.

Violet got into her car and headed toward her shop, knowing everything was perfect for the shoot tomorrow, but still needing to double-check for her own piece of mind. When she pulled into the side lot, she couldn't help but laugh at the old, dilapidated truck that could only have come from Mick's mechanics shop.

Brady was somewhere close by. She sent him a quick text telling him to stop into her shop before he left the area.

Violet let herself in the back door and maneuvered through her boxes of décor and freestanding items. The

Christmas music filtered through from the front and Violet peeked through the door to see a few customers milling about and her trusted employee, Carly, ringing someone up.

Pulling out her cell again, Violet told Brady to come in through the back door. She wanted to speak in private and not disrupt her customers. Her store would be open a few more hours, so she'd let Carly go once Brady left. As crazy as things were right now, Violet still loved her store and helping people choose their favorite decoration or that perfect gift.

Various ideas for Brady's home ran through her mind. She knew the theme, but she really wanted a statement piece and she was racking her brain trying to figure out what she could use.

She opened several boxes, still not finding what she needed. Violet refused to give up. Time was not on her side, but she really wanted something totally unique and special for his home. She wanted him to be glad he agreed to the tour and she wanted him to enjoy this season as much as she did.

The chime on the back door jingled and Violet spun around. Not surprising at all to find Brady with a pair of navy pants and a light gray shirt with the sleeves rolled up.

"Do you wear that lawyer look everywhere?" she asked.

He glanced down and then back to her. "My reindeer pants were in the wash."

Violet couldn't help but laugh at his quick, snarky comeback. "That's why you should always have more than one pair."

"Rookie mistake."

Brady glanced around the room slowly, then let out a low laugh that caused a little dance of arousal deep in her belly. Those dark eyes turned back to her, holding her in place. The chatter from out front and the Christmas music continued, but she might as well be alone with him for the way he was staring at her.

"You wanted to talk?" he asked.

"Oh, yes, I did." She seriously needed to snap out of this spell he had her under. "I had several things I wanted to discuss. First, the magazine crew wants to get inside your house for some photos, but I'd really like it decorated first. So, I need…"

His eyes were wandering again around the room and she realized he wasn't fully listening to her.

"Brady."

He snapped back to her. "What do you do with all of this stuff? I've never seen so many boxes and trees and… hell, everything Christmas."

Violet shrugged. "It's what I do. Most of this stuff is for the tour, but some is back stock for the store. Anyway, as I was saying—"

"Just come by the house later."

Violet blinked. "Excuse me?"

"My house," he said slowly. "That's what you want to discuss, so just come by later. I'll have dinner ready."

Violet crossed her arms over her chest. "Another date?"

His lips quirked. "If that's what you want to call it."

"What do you call it? We eat dinners together, we kiss."

Brady stared at her a minute before taking a step forward. Violet held her breath, keeping her eyes locked on his as he closed the gap between them.

"I don't know what the hell to call this," he admitted, sounding frustrated. "Are you coming over or not?"

Violet smiled. "With a tempting offer like that, how can I refuse?"

Brady took a step back, stared at her once more, and finally nodded a silent agreement before he headed out the back door.

Violet didn't move; she wasn't quite sure what happened or why he seemed angry over this attraction. None of this was her fault—or his really. Things just happened and all she could do now was take this day by day. Clearly ignoring this pull wasn't working.

Blowing out a sigh, Violet turned toward the front of her store. She needed to work, she needed to focus on something she could actually control, and she needed to make sure she didn't lose sight of all of the important things going on around her.

Her mother's wedding, the tour, the magazine interview…there was no room for a love affair.

But that didn't stop her from wanting one.

Chapter Twelve

Christmas calories don't count.
* Violet Calhoun

Brady checked his email once again and was surprised and a little alarmed to find one from the senior partner at the firm. He stared at the unopened message and leaned against the kitchen island.

Did he want to open this now before Violet arrived or did he want to wait?

Considering the message was sent at the end of day on a Friday, Brady wondered if it was bad news. Surely if it was too life changing, someone would have called instead of emailed.

Regardless what the news was, the message wouldn't change no matter when he opened it. Brady tapped on his screen and scanned the words, trying to absorb everything all at once before going back to the top and starting over.

Reading slower this time, Brady digested each and every word. They wanted him back the first Monday of the new year and they wanted him to slide into a trial period of partnership. He had six months before they would ultimately make their decision.

Brady appreciated the statement that commended him on all the work he'd done for them for years and that one setback wouldn't be the deciding factor. He was too valuable as an attorney.

Yet he had six months. He'd been waiting so long to become partner and instead of kicking him completely out for his short temper on one occasion, they were giving him a second chance. A trial, but it was something.

Brady was so damn happy. He would prove to them that once he was rested and relaxed and had this home sold, he could move forward with his life. The stress from his grandfather's passing and the cases he'd been taking on trying to prove himself had definitely taken its toll on his mental state.

But coming back to Peach Grove did something, he couldn't really say what. Maybe it was the hustle and bustle that was so different from the city. This little town definitely had their own way of doing things, but in a manner that made him smile and want to take time to enjoy the day.

How ridiculous did that sound? He'd only been in town a little over a week and was already getting sentimental. He wasn't sure if it was the time of year or the house or maybe even spending time with Violet that made everything seem…well, better.

But all of that was temporary. He wasn't staying here and he couldn't take any of that with him. If he was back in Atlanta right now, he'd likely still be at the office. He never kept "regular" hours like some of his coworkers. Brady pushed himself and maybe that's because his career was his life. What else did he have?

A therapist would seriously have a tough time getting caught in all the twists and turns inside his mind.

The timer went off on the oven and Brady turned everything off and pulled out the pan of lasagna and then the bread. As silly as it sounded, he hoped Violet liked Italian. Other than grilling meat, pasta was about the only thing he could make.

He'd just poured the wine when his doorbell rang. Why the hell he was nervous was beyond him. There was no need to be so tense. They were eating dinner and working on the tour.

Of course the word *date* had been thrown out once again and Brady wished like hell they could keep this a working relationship. Neither of them had the time and he sure as hell didn't have the mental capacity to work on dating someone…or a fling. Because that's all that could happen at this point. He was leaving and her life was most definitely here.

Ignoring the pull in both directions, Brady made his way to the front of the house. As soon as he opened the door, Violet offered him a wide smile and held up a box from Mad Batter.

"I hope you like salted caramel because my bestie makes the best pie ever."

Brady took the box from her and gestured her inside. "I've never had it, but you sent over some of her pastries and they are amazing."

The minute she stepped in, he noticed her shirt and couldn't help but laugh. A bright red shirt with white letters read Dasher, Dancer, Prancer, Vixen, Moscato, Vodka, Tequila, Blitzen.

"I never know what to expect from you," he told her.

"That's quite a compliment," she replied. "I like keeping people on their toes."

She turned her attention toward the end of the hallway and the kitchen. "What smells so amazing? Did you get takeout?"

"Now I'm offended." Brady started back down the hall, Violet right behind him. "I made lasagna. The only thing store bought was the bread."

"Lasagna, I'm impressed."

Even though he wanted her to be, he cursed those giddy feelings that overwhelmed him. Where did this come from? Was he just overworked and lacked a real social life? He'd been forced into this situation so was he falling victim to the circumstances?

His attorney mind kept battling back and forth in a battle he would both lose and win.

"Do you want to eat out on the patio?" he asked.

"Sounds good."

Violet grabbed the wineglasses and headed out back. She'd only been here with him a handful of times, but she was already comfortable, already at home. Something about that unsettled him. He'd never really thought long term as far as relationships went, and he wasn't now. He just couldn't help but wonder if this was how things would be if he had a wife or a girlfriend.

Would he come home from work and they'd cook together or they'd share a drink and unwind from their day?

"Everything okay?"

Violet's question pulled him back and he realized he hadn't even heard her come back in. Brady shook away the crazy thoughts and nodded.

"Just lost in my own mind," he told her. "Go on out and I'll bring the food."

She looked like she wanted to question him further, but she turned and went out to the patio. Brady took a minute to pull himself together. Spending time with a beautiful woman didn't have to be complicated and just because he'd been married to his career didn't mean he couldn't just take a break and reboot his life.

Brady carried the plates out to the table and took a seat across from Violet. The familial setting seemed both foreign and somehow comforting right now. He enjoyed her company, but there was more…a desire that pulled him toward her, a need that he couldn't help but want to explore and uncover the depth.

Sure, the sexual tension was strong, but there was something else he couldn't quite put a label on.

"I haven't made this for quite some time, so I hope it's good," he told her.

"I've never made lasagna and I rarely cook since it's just me."

Brady nodded. "It's easier for me to grab something on the way home from the office. I'm always too tired to do much else in the evenings."

Violet rested her arms on the table and leveled his gaze. "What makes you such a workaholic?"

"Are you the pot or the kettle here?" he asked.

"I love what I do," she told him. "When I come home tired, it's that happy tired. Like I've accomplished something good and had fun. I'm always ready to go the next day."

The passion in her voice was something he didn't recognize. He'd never talked about his job like this, never came home with that happy exhaustion. He didn't even know what the hell that meant.

Violet took a bite of her dinner and let out a moan. Her lids lowered and she let out another low moan that did nothing to help squelch that growing desire.

"I'll assume by your reaction that it's good," he chuckled.

Her eyes focused back on him as she nodded. "It's amazing. I can't believe you made this."

"Yeah, well, don't get too excited. My culinary skills are limited. This is one of the things I remember my grandmother making. She let me help in the kitchen until she got to the point she couldn't cook anymore."

More memories of his childhood came flooding back. The summers he spent here were some of the best moments of his entire life. He couldn't help but smile.

"She was a special lady," Violet told him. "You were blessed to have such role models in your life."

"They were amazing," he agreed. "You always hear the saying you don't know what you had until it's gone, and that is something you don't fully grasp until it happens to you."

Violet tipped her head and offered a soft grin. "I have to confess that I sort of self-adopted William as my own grandfather a few years ago. I never knew my grandparents and once we started working on the tour committee together, we just clicked."

That unwanted twinge of guilt hit him hard once again. He'd been so busy working toward a partnership, building his career and wanting to be strong like his father in a corporate world, he'd let time slip by and now there was no more time with those who shaped his life.

"I'm glad mine could be here for you," he told her. "And thanks for being there for my grandpa these past few years."

"I'm not sure who really helped whom," she admitted. "We seemed to rely on each other. I would sometimes bring takeout and we'd brainstorm over dinner. We'd always talk about the tour, but then we'd end up chatting about everything else. He was a great listener. Not too many people are."

"You are."

The words were out of his mouth before he realized he'd even had the thought, but it was true. Violet might be quirky and she was annoying as hell at first. But she cared, and those were the people who actually listened and wanted to be a shoulder to lean on.

"Thanks. Sometimes I talk too much," she told him with a slight grin. "So what about your parents? William talked about his son, but not often."

Brady sat back in his seat and sighed. "There was always some disconnect between my grandfather and my dad. My dad always had a bigger vision, bigger goals than to stay here. He wanted a city life, something fast paced. He was all business and always so serious."

"Sounds totally opposite of William."

Brady nodded. "They were. I guess I'm just a healthy mix of the two."

"Yet you haven't been here in years, other than the funeral."

Yeah, that was the niggling guilt that had plagued him for months.

"I have regrets," he admitted, then blew out a sigh. "But let's talk about something else. What's the theme for my house? I'm almost afraid to know."

Violet pursed her lips, then smiled so wide, that punch of lust hit him once again. Damn, she was a striking woman with that mass of curly hair and bright eyes. There was something so wholesome and sweet about her, but when she stared at him with those heavy lids, he couldn't help but think of her in a much more intimate setting.

"I really want it to be a surprise," she told him. "But I might need to incorporate your help."

Brady laughed. "How would it be a surprise and I still help you?"

"Well, you can help me pull in the decorations and set up, but there's one big element I'm keeping to myself until the end."

"So is this a surprise for the tour or the magazine folks?" he asked.

Violet tipped her head in that familiar way he was finding all too adorable. A stray curl fell across her forehead and she shoved it aside.

"The surprise is for you," she told him. "I want you to love this as much as I do and I want you to be happy you chose to keep this house on the tour."

She wanted to surprise him? Nobody ever surprised him. He didn't do things like that or even gifts. For Christmas, he ordered his personal assistant the same box of chocolate-covered fruit every single year. That was the extent of the surprises in his life.

When had anyone ever done something like this for him?

"Are you all right?" she asked, her brows drawing inward.

Brady nodded. "Yeah, fine. I'm just…confused."

"Because I'm keeping this a surprise?"

"Yes."

"Then you need more spontaneous things in your life," she told him. "Doesn't anybody ever just do something for you in the spur of the moment or something that takes you off guard?"

"Never."

Violet stared at him for a minute, then she busted out laughing. "Well, good thing you met me. We're about to change that."

"Excuse me?"

She grabbed the napkin off her lap and tossed it onto the table. Then she drained her glass of wine and came to her feet.

"Let's go."

Brady stared up at her. "Go where?"

"That's a surprise."

He raked a hand over his jaws, the stubble bristling against his palm. That was new, too. He hadn't shaved for a couple days when in his normal world he did so every single morning before heading into the office.

"Listen, you're supposed to be here to relax," she told him. "I say having fun and being spontaneous goes with that. You need to loosen up a little."

"I am loose," he volleyed back. "I'm not wearing a suit."

"But you had one on earlier, so it doesn't count. Now, let's go."

Knowing that fighting with her wasn't going to get him anywhere, and he was quite intrigued, Brady stood and gestured for her to go.

"I'll follow," he said. "Are we walking or driving?"

"It's a nice night. You up for a walk?"

Brady smiled...something he'd been doing quite a bit around her. He hadn't realized just how stressed and overworked he'd been until Violet. She was refreshing and now she was taking him for a walk. He had no clue where they were going, but there was something old-school romantic about a bright moon and a starry evening and heading down his tree-lined drive toward the road.

He wasn't looking for romance, wasn't looking for a fling or anything of the sort. And while he wasn't looking… Brady worried that's exactly what he was finding.

Chapter Thirteen

I just want to drink hot chocolate and watch
Christmas movies.
* Violet Calhoun

Violet walked side by side with Brady, wondering if he felt comfortable or awkward. Somehow this stroll through the town seemed like a date. On the other hand, she felt like they were old friends.

Even though he'd come to town when he'd been younger, Violet really didn't know him. But the strong bond they both shared with William tied them together by default. At least, that's what she first thought. Now, though, she knew there was so much more and she wanted to continue to explore.

She led him toward the entrance to the park, feeling a little schoolgirlish with her wayward thoughts. Confidence had never been a problem for her, yet she wondered if Brady felt the same.

Part of her assumed he did since he'd initiated that last kiss. Violet found that aggression rather sexy, though knowing what she did about Brady, he likely planned the kiss rather than being spontaneous. She always went after what she wanted, so he better hold on for the ride.

But how did she want Brady? She really didn't know how this would continue or where she thought their encounters would actually go. But she found that when she was with him, she didn't want the time to end.

"I always love walking here at night," she admitted. "Everything is so peaceful and calm."

"Peaceful and calm don't typically live in my world."

Violet laughed. "No, I don't imagine they do. That's why I brought you here. Come on. I'll show you my favorite spot."

She reached for his hand and pulled him deeper into the park. The moment she laced her fingers with his, she wondered if she'd gone too far, but he held on and a new burst of attraction coursed through her.

Her feelings were quite an unexpected jumble. Between the initial attraction, the sexual awareness, those kisses that curled her toes, and now the sweetness of holding hands—she was letting nothing else in but the happiness of being with Brady.

Maybe she was foolish for wanting more from him, knowing he wasn't staying and knowing she didn't have time to feed into a relationship. She hadn't dated for so long, and she hadn't really been looking to date, either. But she couldn't ignore this strong pull of desire and the way he made her feel. Doing so wouldn't be fair...to either of them.

"I used to come to the park with my grandfather for the summer festival when I was younger," Brady told her. "I had my first corn dog here. I also had my first kiss when I was thirteen."

Violet laughed. "Sounds like you have some good memories."

"Memories I had forgotten about until now," he admitted. "Those were good times that I guess just got shoved to the back of my mind as adulthood and life took over."

"We still have the festival." She led him down another stone path through the lush flower gardens. "I actually work on that committee as well."

"Of course you do."

"I like to stay busy and help where I can," she told him. "This town had gotten so run down, businesses closed and jobs were leaving. It was depressing seeing all of those old buildings boarded up."

"You should be proud of the work you and your friends have done."

Between the strength of his hand and the compliment, Violet couldn't help but smile. Brady was a special guy and she was seeing more and more just how much so.

"I am proud of all of our hard work," she replied, guiding him down another path. "We each knew we had skills and strengths. We took risks, used our savings, and dove into being business owners. None of us really had any extra money for marketing or anything fancy. Word of mouth is what fueled us."

"That's the most effective tool for any business. It can make or break you."

They reached the white gazebo and Violet stepped up, releasing Brady's hand as he came in behind her.

"We're doing a photo shoot here in the morning for the magazine." She took a seat on one of the curved benches. "I mentioned the gazebo because it's such a special place for this town. We have weddings here, we have concerts from local talent, this is where the mayor takes his oath. I just couldn't imagine a more perfect spot."

"I remember seeing a local band play here during the festival," he stated, coming to stand beside her.

"As much as I love this place during the day when there're so many families and kids and people walking through, my favorite time is at night when all is quiet and I can just decompress."

"I knew even you couldn't go at lightning speed all hours of the day." He laughed.

Silence surrounded them for a moment. There was so much peace and something comforting about sharing this spot with him. She'd never brought a guy here or told anyone that she used this area for her downtime and to reboot her mind.

Violet glanced up to see Brady's eyes up toward the sky. "The stars are bright," she told him. "I bet you don't get this beautiful view in Atlanta."

He glanced over his shoulder. "I have a view from my balcony, but nothing like this. The sky seems so much larger out here, the stars more vibrant."

"What got you so interested in astronomy?"

His focus shifted back to the sky. "I had to take a few electives in college and I took astronomy classes. When I was younger and would visit here in the summers, my grandfather had a telescope he set up on the second-story porch. We would always look at the stars and he would tell me what little he knew. I just always found it so fascinating. One day I tripped and the telescope fell over and broke into several pieces. If he ever replaced it, I didn't know about it."

Violet knew. She didn't know all of this backstory, but she did know about William owning a telescope and she knew right where it was.

"Do you have a telescope at home?" she asked, keeping her thoughts and her new plans to herself.

He shook his head. "I've never bought one. I always

think I should, but then I just get busy and it slips my mind."

"Has it crossed your mind that you work too much?" she asked. "And, yes, I know I work like crazy, but you and I are quite different."

He laughed and turned to face her. "I'm well aware of how different we are."

The wind kicked up a little, blowing random, wavy strands in front of her face. She should've grabbed a holder to pull it all back, but she hadn't really thought about it. Lately her thoughts were either on Christmas or Brady and not her unruly hair.

She tucked her hair behind her ears and stared up at him. "Do you have a place at home that you can just relax and get away? Or does your volunteer time do that for you?"

"I enjoy the planetarium." He shrugged a shoulder. "I guess I've never really thought about anything more. I go to the office and then home. Sometimes I have appointments that take me to a client or I'll get together with colleagues for a drink, but that's about it."

She wondered if he knew how lonely that sounded. If he ever considered having a social life or taking a break from what obviously wore him down. If he ever created a personal bond that had nothing whatsoever to do with work.

"What brought you here?" she asked. "Other than going through William's things."

Brady raked a hand over the back of his neck and turned to pace. "Stress got to me. That's the short version."

"And the long story?" She desperately wanted to

know, but she wouldn't push if he wasn't ready or willing to share.

Brady faced her once again, resting his hands on his hips. "I was like a boiling pot. It was only a matter of time before I exploded, but I didn't realize it until it was too late. I had guilt from Granddad's passing and being absent for so long, I was overworked and stretched too thin. I blew up on another attorney before a court hearing and I was removed from the case."

"Yikes."

"Exactly. I was told in no uncertain terms to take a break until the first of the year. I've never displayed that type of behavior before, so everyone pretty much gave me a pass. I didn't know what the hell I would do without working, so I decided to come here. I couldn't put off going through the house any longer. I was hoping for closure or something, but all I have is more mixed emotions than ever."

No wonder he hadn't been in the mood for her when he arrived. He'd been dealt quite a bit over the last few months and was just now coping with it all. On top of that, she came busting into his life assuming he would comply with her demands.

"Sorry if I've been pushy."

He looked at her for a moment before he let out a burst of laughter. "You? Pushy? More like you steamrolled me."

Violet shrugged. "I take my work seriously and, if I'm honest, the Jackson estate has always been my favorite. As a little girl I would dream of what it would be like to live there. Once I started working with the tour and getting hands-on experience with decorating the home, my fantasies ran wild. I would give anything to have that place for myself."

"Where do you live?" he asked.

"In the apartment over top of my business. Robin and Simone live above their shops, too. That's another way we were able to buy our buildings. We sold our homes and just decided to live in the lofts."

"That's pretty remarkable."

Violet came to her feet and sighed. "Some people told us we were taking too much of a chance, some said we were stubborn. In my opinion, we were determined. None of us wanted to leave this town and we thought if we banded together and brought businesses that people would actually use, then maybe others would take a chance and open more old storefronts."

Brady took a step toward her, his dark eyes never wavering, and she wondered what he was thinking... and what he was doing. The way he looked at her made Violet both intrigued and aroused. She'd never noticed a man looking at her with such longing before.

Or if a man did, she didn't notice it.

"You wanted to make a difference," he stated simply. "It's amazing what someone can do when they refuse to lose and don't give up."

"I've never given up on anything," she admitted with a grin. "Just wait until you see what I have planned for your house."

"You can't give me a hint?"

Violet thought for a minute and replied, "It has to do with Santa, but that's all I'm saying."

"Santa?" He seemed legitimately confused as he drew his brows in. "Is it too late to tell you I don't believe in Santa?"

"As long as you believe in the magic of Christmas, that's all I care about."

Brady said nothing as he just continued to stare at her.

"You do believe this time of year is magical, don't you?"

"I never thought of it in terms of being magical."

Violet reached up and patted his cheek. "That's where we need to fix you."

She realized her mistake a second too late. Brady reached up and covered her hand, flattening her palm against the stubble on his jaw.

"Is that what you're trying to do?" he asked, his voice low and husky. "Fix me?"

Violet swallowed. "I don't want to change you, but maybe just open your eyes."

His eyes dipped to her mouth. "Oh, they're open."

The moment his head dipped, Violet tipped her chin and opened for him. His hands came up and framed her face, his thumbs stroking along her jawline. Violet gripped his biceps as she held on and let Brady take what he wanted.

Her hips lined up with his, their torsos pressed together. Violet arched against him and relished the strength and warmth and passion. He had so much to offer, so much she wanted from him.

A whining in the distance pulled Violet from her thoughts and the moment. Brady eased back, obviously hearing the strange sound, too.

The noise echoed once again, a little louder this time.

"I'm assuming that wasn't you," he said.

Violet laughed. "That was a good kiss, but no, not me."

The sound came once again, only closer this time. Violet released Brady as they both started to look around.

The lampposts from the sidewalks helped to illuminate the area, but Violet still didn't see anything. Brady stepped out of the gazebo and started looking around the bushes along the perimeter.

He stooped down and reached his hand out. "Hey, little guy."

Violet moved closer and tried to see what was in there.

"Come on," Brady urged in a soft tone. "It's okay. I won't hurt you."

"What is it?"

Brady glanced over his shoulder. "A puppy."

He leaned in a little farther and reached with both hands. "I think he's stuck in the bottom of this bush."

Violet dropped to her knees and pulled out her phone from her pocket, turning on the flashlight so Brady could see better. Little brown eyes stared back at her. The tiny furball was all black and looked terrified.

"Almost got him," Brady said. "There."

He pulled out the pup and held him against his chest. Violet put her phone away and gently reached to pet the shivering baby.

"He's adorable," she said, leaning closer to get a better look at him. "He doesn't have a collar on, though."

"Do you think he just wandered off or did someone dump him here?"

Violet leaned closer, loving the smell of puppies and wanting the little guy to feel safe. "I don't know. We can take him back to your house and I can get a few pictures of him to post on social media and see if anyone is missing him."

Violet started to reach for him, but he burrowed his head against Brady's neck. The little guy still trembled, and seeing Brady's large hands comfort the puppy was so adorable, Violet couldn't help but smile.

"Looks like you're his favorite," she said.

"Only because I freed his leg from the bush. Let's get him home and make sure he's okay."

Violet wished they would've driven instead of walked, but they made it back to Brady's house twenty minutes later and set the pup on the floor in the entryway. He was even bigger than she'd first thought, but up against Brady's chest the dog seemed small.

Brady got down on the floor and Violet sat beside him.

"He doesn't seem to be limping or anything," Brady muttered as his hands gently moved over the dog. "We should call the vet and see if anyone called in a missing dog. I'll do that if you want to take those pictures."

Violet pulled out her cell and snapped some pics up close and quickly posted them online. She hoped she didn't get a flood of people claiming this was their dog. Thankfully he had a little white marking on his belly so she'd just have to ask questions to make sure whoever claimed him knew of the special spot.

"You're a good boy." Violet ran her hand down the dog's soft coat. "We'll find your home."

The pup squatted and promptly peed all over the hardwood and Violet hopped up and ran to get some paper towels. By the time she came back, the little guy was attempting to climb the stairs…and failing. His little furry butt dangled from the bottom step and Violet scooped him up. He flopped onto his back, paws up by his little face…and that's when Violet realized he was actually a she.

"Well, you are quite a little handful, you stinker."

She set the puppy back down and finished wiping up the mess.

"I left a message with the emergency number at the vet," Brady said as he came back in.

"Can you watch her? I need to wash my hands. She had an accident on your floor."

"She?"

Violet nodded. "I found out the obvious way." She laughed. "Be right back."

Once she tossed the soiled paper towels, washed her hands, and came back, she found Brady on the floor with the little pup pouncing on his chest and trying to bite his nose. Her heart flipped in her chest and she wasn't sure she'd seen a more adorable sight in her life.

Not only was Brady intelligent, sexy, an exceptional kisser, he was also an animal lover and that said a great deal about the true side of this man she barely knew...yet she felt like she'd known him her whole life.

"Looks like you have a new best friend."

Brady glanced over with a smile on his face, one she hadn't seen before. His entire face seemed to light up as the pup licked his chin.

"I didn't even know I was looking for one," he told her.

Violet pulled out her cell again and looked to her social media to see if anyone had responded about the dog. So far the only comments were about how cute and furry she was.

"Hopefully the vet knows something," she told Brady. "I'm sure some little kid is missing their new puppy. And no doubt this was an early Christmas present."

"But she doesn't have a collar." Brady rolled over onto his belly and the dog pounced onto his back. "She's really playful."

Violet squatted down and ran her hand between the dog's ears. "What should we call her?"

Brady gave her a side-glance. "Call her?"

"A name."

"We can't name her. She's not ours."

"No, but she's yours right now."

The dog pounced off his back and Brady sat up. "She's not mine," he told her. "I don't know anything about keeping a dog and I'm sure someone will claim her soon."

"Well, you need to keep her until then," she told him. "How about I run and get some food, bowls, and a leash?"

"Wait. What?"

The dog crawled over his lap and circled him. Then she started nibbling on his shoe before barking and pouncing, then trying to chew once again. Clearly she wanted to play.

Violet laughed. "I'll add chew toy to my list."

She came to her feet and Brady rose with her, his eyes wide as he glanced from the dog to her.

"What am I supposed to do with her until you get back?" he asked, suddenly sounding panicked.

"Pet her, take her out back to play, get her a bowl of water. I won't be gone long."

Violet grabbed her purse from the table beside the door and left before Brady could panic any further. Part of her thought this was good for him. Nothing would make him lighten up quicker than a rambunctious puppy.

But if nobody stepped forward, then what would happen? Brady wasn't staying and she was never home enough to care for an animal. Hopefully someone would claim the puppy soon.

Chapter Fourteen

*If anyone wants to get me a Christmas present, I'm a
size window seat and tropical island.*
* Violet Calhoun

The ringing persisted and Brady started to reach out to
the table for his cell. But the lump on his back was proof
the puppy had finally worn herself out and fallen asleep.

Brady decided to remain still. No way in hell did he
want to rouse the beast. Who knew such a little thing
could have so much energy?

The cell finally stopped ringing and the alert for a
voicemail took its place. He'd check it later. He honestly
had no clue what time he finally fell asleep on the couch,
but he was just thankful that Violet had brought back sup-
plies. The dog had loved the chew toy to death…literally.
There were threads and stuffing everywhere from what
used to be a stuffed monkey.

Maybe Violet had heard something from the rightful
owner. Someone knew where this puppy came from, now
if they would just come forward. Unless they didn't want
the dog, in which case that would be an entirely different scenario…and that would make someone an absolute
jerk to treat an animal this way.

His doorbell rang and Brady jerked, blinking against the bright living room. Had he fallen asleep again?

The dog popped up and barked, then fell off Brady's back and onto the floor. Just as he started to see if she was okay, the pup scrambled toward the entryway and was barking her fool head off.

Brady came to his feet and rubbed a hand through his hair. His stiff back and sore neck were not happy about sleeping on the sofa. He hadn't meant to. He'd lain down for a minute with the dog until he'd ultimately passed out.

The doorbell rang once more, sending the dog into an even louder, higher pitched barking fit.

Brady reached down to lift the dog so she didn't run out the door before he flicked the lock. The second the door swung open, Violet stood there with a wide smile.

"Oh, did I wake you?" she asked, raking her eyes over him. "It's almost noon."

"Noon? Seriously?"

Violet let herself in and laughed. "Rough night with your new girlfriend?"

He closed the door and set the dog down. She immediately went and started jumping up at Violet's legs… which he noticed were nice and bare.

"Luna, get down."

Violet quirked her brow. "Luna. That's cute. I didn't think you were naming her."

Brady twisted his neck from side to side to get the kink out. "I can't keep calling her dog or pup. I had to do something."

"That's adorable."

He didn't want to be adorable. He wanted to sleep in his bed without a furball on his back.

"Why are you so dressed up?" he asked, snapping his fingers to get Luna's attention.

"I had the photo shoot, remember? Robin, Simone, and I were at the gazebo in the park and we ended up going to each of our buildings and getting a few shots, too."

Her simple red dress with short sleeves and her little gold sandals were adorable. She was dressed up without being over the top and tacky. She'd done something to those crazy curls and they were now tame and calm. Brady realized he'd gotten used to the quirky way she dressed and that mass of dark red hair. This new look seemed almost…not Violet.

The puppy started circling and Brady rushed to her, picking her up, and carrying her out to the backyard. He was just in time. The second he set her down, she squatted and did her business.

From the open doorway behind him, Violet's laughter filtered out.

"So how's the potty training?" she asked.

Brady glanced over his shoulder and found her leaning against the doorframe with a wide smile on her face. Her hair hung down around one shoulder and she had the slightest bit of makeup on. He couldn't get over how she'd transformed into someone else, someone more polished and put together.

Crazy to even think, but he definitely preferred the old Violet.

"Have any luck with your posting?" he asked.

Violet stepped out of the house and came on out to the patio area. She shook her head and sighed. "Nothing. Any luck from the vet?"

"They were supposed to call if they heard a report

about a missing dog," he said as he watched Luna pounce around the yard.

"So, what are you going to do?" Violet asked.

Brady stared at the dog bouncing through the yard, diving into the landscaping, and trying to chew mulch. The little thing was so damn rotten, but he couldn't help but love her.

"I have no idea," he admitted honestly. "I can't keep a dog. I've got to go through the stuff in the house, you have to start decorating, I'll be leaving on New Year's Day. There's just so much going on."

Luna hopped over the taller blades of grass and came to sit at his feet. Then the little furball stared up at him like she knew what they were discussing.

"She's trying to guilt me," he muttered.

Violet came to stand beside him and snickered. "I'd say she's doing a good job. You know animals tend to find their person. Looks like you are Luna's person."

"I can't be her person," he insisted. "I can't be."

"Yet you gave her a name."

He shot her a side eye. "I'm not keeping her."

Violet merely raised a brow and smiled, like she knew something he didn't. She could give him a knowing smile all she wanted, but they had to find the rightful owner.

"I meant to ask last night how the study is coming along." Violet turned to face him as she tucked her hair behind her ears. "Still need my help?"

"If you're offering, I won't turn it down. Aren't you too busy with your store, your mother's wedding, the magazine, and the tour?" Brady waited a second for a reaction, but when he got none, he went on. "You don't think you have enough going on without helping me go through papers and pictures?"

"My store is covered, my mother isn't getting married today, your house is on the tour so I'm technically still working on it, and I'm done with the magazine people today. They are with Robin."

Brady bit the inside of his jaw to keep from smiling. "Sounds like you have all the answers."

"I wouldn't have offered if I didn't want to help," she told him. "You know how much I love this house and how much I loved William."

He couldn't help himself. Brady took a step closer until she tipped her head up to look him in the eyes.

"Are those the only reasons you offered to help?" he asked.

"Do you need me to admit I like spending time with you?" Her smile widened. "I didn't take you as someone who needed their ego stroked, remember?"

The woman could drive him out of his mind, but he couldn't help but laugh. He'd never met someone so bold, which was saying a great deal considering he worked in a law firm and dealt with divorce for a living.

"Fine," he conceded. "I'll forgo the compliment for some help in the study."

"Let me run home and change and I'll be back." She glanced down to Luna, who was bouncing around their feet. "Maybe let her play out here for a while and wear her out. She might sleep while we're working."

"How do you know so much about dogs?" he asked.

"I had a dog growing up. Didn't you?"

Brady shook his head. "Dad wouldn't allow it."

"That's not right," she stated. "Every kid deserves a pet. It teaches responsibility and there's a bond you make that stays with you forever."

Every time she opened her mouth, Brady found her

more and more intriguing. He realized he wanted to learn everything about her and he worried there wasn't enough time to uncover all that made up Violet Calhoun.

"Better go get changed," he told her. "We have work to do."

"He's infuriating," Robin hissed.

Violet hurried around the back room of her store, looking for anything and everything to take to Brady's house. She'd spent all evening helping Brady go through more boxes and they'd made quite a dent. Not only had they shared a few stories as the memories flowed, they'd also stolen a few kisses here and there. And Luna had, for the most part, kept to the new rubber chew toy and an old sock Violet had brought back for her.

"I don't know why this is so difficult for you," Violet said, pulling a box down from the top shelf.

She had Robin on speakerphone as she climbed up and down on her small stepladder trying to get everything together. Clearly her friend needed to talk, but Violet only had so many hands.

"Because he's so damn arrogant," Robin cried. "He wouldn't know a petunia from a lily. He tried to tell me how I should display the arrangement for the photos yesterday evening."

"We took several photos already," Violet reminded her. "He wanted more?"

"When Lauren interviewed me on my own, he came along and took some candid shots," she explained. "I mean, how many photos can the guy need?"

"I didn't realize he was coming with Lauren."

"Yeah, well, neither did I," Robin grumbled. "The

man is a photographer, not a florist. I didn't try to tell him how to do his job, did I? No."

Violet listened as her friend droned on and on. Sometimes it was best to just listen and say nothing. At least, that's what Vi hoped her friend needed. Violet's own mind was too consumed with making Brady's home absolutely perfect, not to mention the rolling to-do list for her mom's wedding. Everything was happening all at once and the excitement and anticipation just kept Violet going on autopilot.

"Well, perhaps you're done with him for a while," Violet told her friend. "They should do an exclusive with Simone next. I know they're planning on being at the chocolate walk next week to interview some of the people from the town and to get more photos."

"Didn't you have an issue with him?" Robin asked.

"None at all."

"Then why me?"

Violet lifted the lid from the box and found exactly what she needed for the staircase at Brady's. Now if she could just find that garland of clear stars.

"I mean, Bryce is pretty handsome," Violet stated. "Do you think the irritability is stemming from attraction? Maybe you two just rub each other the wrong way."

"Attraction?" Robin scoffed. "Are you out of your mind?"

"You don't think he's cute?"

"If I could get beyond the fact he irritates me, then maybe I could appreciate his looks."

Violet didn't think there was any way any woman with a heartbeat could ignore how hot Bryce was. But, on the other hand, Vi figured she was in trouble because nobody got her schoolgirl giddiness up like Brady Jackson.

"Listen, I need to run," Violet said. "I'm heading to Brady's to officially start the tour decorating."

"With some volunteers?"

Violet stared at the phone sitting on the table and pursed her lips. She could lie, but that never was her style. "No. I'm a little territorial with this house."

Robin laughed. "Don't you mean the man?"

"Uh…"

"Please, don't deny it." Robin continued to chuckle, but quickly sobered and let out a sigh. "Just be careful, please. You know Simone said he was married to his job, plus he's not staying. He doesn't even want to be here at all."

Yet he was settling in and growing more accustomed to the town each day. Would he want to stay? Would he find reasons to come back more often? Maybe he would have a change of heart and keep the house.

Her mind was running wild with naïve thoughts and she didn't have the time for childish daydreams.

"I'm careful," Violet promised. "I'll talk to you later."

Once she hung up, she checked with Carly to make sure everything was good with the store and then she loaded up her Jeep with all the boxes she could cram inside. She'd definitely have to make more trips and check the storage unit because she was missing all of those strands of garland she wanted to use along the outside rails for the two porches.

The stars, the silver shimmer, the touches of blue accents, garland, wreaths…all of that was perfect for her theme and her visions, but every home had one big "aha" thing that made it stand out. There was only one thing that would make this special for the town and for Brady.

When all of this was over, she was going to need a vacation. As much as she loved her job and her volunteer work and planning for her mother, come December 26th, she needed to decompress and clear her mind.

The moment Violet pulled into Brady's drive, she stopped her Jeep and just stared straight ahead. There was nothing more Southern or more breathtaking than this image right here. It could be a postcard or the opening credits to a Hallmark movie.

The Jackson plantation going up for sale was absolutely unimaginable and completely heartbreaking. Violet was already jealous of the new owners. Would they even appreciate this place the way she did? Would they act like a child and swing on the tire swing? Maybe unwind at the end of the day with a glass of wine on the enclosed second-story porch off the back of the master suite?

Would they grow a family here and have picnics and summer cookouts with friends? Maybe an ice cream social or something just as fancy and fun.

Violet cursed herself for letting her daydream carry her away. This would get her nowhere and longing for the impossible would only make things worse in the long run. She was literally asking for heartache. There wasn't a chance in hell she could afford the mortgage on a place like this. She loved her little loft apartment. She lived alone and what she had was more than adequate. Even if she had the money, what would she do with a giant plantation home? The cleaning alone would keep her swamped.

Getting back to reality and the task at hand, Violet put her car in Drive and focused on things she could actually control.

Well, some of this she could control. The tour and the

decorating was all good, but her growing feelings for the guy just passing through could prove to be problematic.

Looked like heartache was going to come in one form or another.

Chapter Fifteen

Everyone gets my opinion this year for Christmas.
Get excited.
* Violet Calhoun

Brady stood back and stared at the boxes and totes and bags that now covered the majority of his entryway. He had no clue how Violet managed to get all of this in here with only making two trips with her Jeep.

"Do you have to use all this stuff with every house?" he asked.

"Depends on the house." Violet rested her hands on her hips. "Your house is substantially larger than some. But the décor also depends on theme. Sometimes I use large pieces, like the giant nutcrackers or the massive sled I've used in a front yard. Other times it's the small details that really make the house. One time I used a live children's choir. It was absolutely spectacular."

Brady listened to her talk and once again, she had such passion in her voice. He'd never met anyone who loved their job like this woman. She was remarkable on so many levels.

Luna came jingling and bouncing into the room, sniffing each box.

"Hey, there, cutie," Violet cooed as she squatted down to pet the pup. "Are you still keeping your daddy awake?"

"I'm not her daddy," he grumbled.

Violet flashed him a smile over her shoulder. "Then what label do I give you? Foster dad? Caregiver? Best friend? Pooper scooper?"

He shot her a glare. "I'm still waiting on the owner to come forward," he replied.

Violet stood and sighed, clearly trying not to laugh at his predicament. "I'd say we both know that if someone was going to come forward, they would have done so by now. I'm afraid Luna was either dumped or ran away, and wherever she came from, they don't want her back."

"Well, how the hell can I keep her? I'm not cut out for owning a pet."

Violet reached over and patted his cheek like a child. "And yet here you are, doing a stellar job of owning a pet. Luna loves it here and she loves you."

He growled and shook his head. "I couldn't just leave her outside to fend for herself. I would never do something like that."

"I know you wouldn't," she told him with a soft smile that kicked him right in the gut.

Why did she have to be so damn perfect? He didn't want perfect. He didn't want anything except to get back to the job he'd worked his entire adult life to build.

That's where he wanted the perfect in his life. He wanted to go back to the firm, forget there was ever a blowup, and move on to becoming the best divorce attorney in the area.

Somehow, though, he seemed to be moving farther away from that goal and heading toward something he didn't recognize.

"That's why you're perfect for Luna," Violet went on. "She adores you. I'm sure you could do something with her when you went back to Atlanta, couldn't you?"

"I live in a condo," he told her. "She needs a yard to run around in and I'm rarely home. I can't even keep a houseplant alive."

Violet rolled her eyes and came to her feet. "I'm sure there's someone who can help you. An elderly neighbor or a doggy day care in that fancy city of yours."

Brady stared at her, wondering if she truly thought that would work. His lifestyle was too hectic and nothing about it would be fair to the dog. Not to mention the fact that a serious, long-term commitment terrified him... not that he'd ever admit that out loud.

"I could look into the day care," he muttered, not really keen on the idea of Luna in a place with a bunch of other dogs. "Let's not worry about that right now. What are the plans for the day and all this decorating you want me to help with?"

Violet continued to stare at him like she wanted to keep discussing the arrangements for Luna, but she finally turned her attention back to the stacks of boxes and bags in his foyer.

"What we need to do is arrange the furniture in the front living room and in the family living room. The rest of the first floor works, but I need a good flow for the foot traffic that will be coming through."

She started into the front room, muttering under her breath and pointing in various directions. Apparently she didn't need his input as she seemed to be having a full-on conversation with herself. Then she took the wreath down that she'd just put up only the other day. She held on to it as she continued to work things out and have a one-person staff meeting.

"Okay," she announced, turning toward him. "I have a plan, but I'm going to need reinforcements. Let me run a couple errands to grab some more things and then I'll be back with Porter."

"Porter?"

Violet nodded. "He always helps me when I need to move things."

Offended, Brady pointed to himself. "I'm right here. Just tell me what you need done."

"I figured you could watch the dog."

"I have a small kennel for her."

Violet jerked back. "You went out to get a kennel?"

"I called Dwight at the hardware store and he brought me one. We used to play together during the summers as kids."

"Well, you are one step ahead of me."

Brady didn't know why her wide smile and obvious approval gave him a little ego boost. She'd been wrong those times she'd accused him of not needing the boost. He felt like a damn teenager trying to impress the popular girl.

"Let me get Luna in her kennel with her toys. I'll be right back."

Brady took the toys and scooped up Luna then headed up to his bedroom where he'd put the kennel and a soft bed. By the time he came back downstairs, Violet had already moved a couple of accent tables around and was standing in the wide doorway separating the dining area from the formal living area.

He didn't even get to ask what she wanted him to do. Violet went into straight work mode, ordering him around and directing where things should now be located. During all of the moving and lifting—in which he noted exactly how strong she was—he couldn't help but realize just how damn sexy her commanding presence was. Who knew he found that quality attractive?

As if he needed another reason to be drawn to her.

"Okay," she said on a sigh as she stood back and surveyed their work. "I think this will definitely work. If you want to take a break and let Luna out, I'll start getting the decorations into this room."

"Why don't we both take a break and I can take her out and then we can grab some lunch?"

"Are you cooking again?"

Brady shrugged. "We could go to that little café I saw on Cherry Lane."

"Corner Café? They have the best wraps." Violet pursed her lips. "Will Luna be okay by herself that long?"

"I've never left her alone," he replied. "I assume."

"How about this," Violet offered. "You let Luna out and I'll go pick up food and bring it back."

"I can go get the food. I have a box of books to drop off at the library next door."

Violet took the clip from her hair and twisted everything back up and adjusted the clip back in. So much hair and he absolutely loved it. The color, the craziness... everything. She was a striking woman without a stitch of makeup or getting fussed up.

"I can do it," she offered. "I'll place our order, then drop off the books, and then I'll go back and get the food. Give me about a half hour."

He figured letting her go might be best. The last thing he wanted was to run into more people who wanted to talk about his grandfather. The man was well loved and

Brady enjoyed all the stories, but they also made him sad and he just didn't want anything to ruin his day with Violet. Never in his wildest dreams did he ever think he'd not only give in to her madness but also be assisting her.

Clearly he'd lost his mind. Either that or this infatuation was causing him to make rash decisions.

"I'll get the boxes and load them into your Jeep," he told her. "Be right back."

Brady retrieved the boxes, got them loaded, and told Vi to order anything for him so long as it had meat and didn't have mayo. He wasn't too picky.

After she left, he got Luna from her kennel and took her out onto the patio so she could run off some energy. The pup was either off or on, there was no in between.

His thoughts shifted ahead to when he went back home and he pulled out his phone to look up doggy day cares. Was he really going to do this? Was he really considering taking in an animal? Who knew how big this dog would get. Hell, he wasn't even sure if his building allowed pets. When he'd moved in, that had been a nonissue. Just another thing he'd have to look into.

As he watched Luna bounce around the yard and tumble over the landscaping, he couldn't help but feel an attachment. And the cute, boisterous pup wasn't the only one he was getting attached to.

He still had seven weeks to go and he knew his attraction and bond to Violet would only grow deeper. That was something else he'd have to deal with entirely. A dog was one thing, but the woman was another.

Now what the hell did he do?

When Violet finished delivering the boxes of books, she couldn't help but walk through the old three-story library. She loved the smell of old books, or books in general, really. There was still another ten minutes before her order would be ready next door so she found herself going to the top floor where the history section was located... and where the key to Brady's house décor was located.

Violet trailed her fingers around the old marble banister that made a perfect square in the middle of the floor to allow people to look down onto the first floor. As she headed to the local history area, her favorite, she came to an abrupt halt.

There it was. William's telescope, which he'd donated to the library just before he passed.

With a rush of excitement, Violet went to track down a worker. She knew a few of them, so hopefully it would not be a problem to borrow the one perfect item that would make Brady fall in love with this house and this tour.

Making Brady's home the center of attention was her main goal. She was surprised he'd gotten on board so easily...well, after some persuasion. But he was joining in and actually seemed a little less grouchy about the whole ordeal.

But, as excited as she was about the tour, she wasn't looking forward to staging the home to sell. Staging would be a joy, but it was the aftereffect that she wasn't so keen on. She wanted that home to stay in the Jackson name. The Jackson mansion had never had anyone else live there except a family member.

She couldn't tell Brady what to do. He had to live his own life and do what worked best for him. But she wished like hell he'd reconsider. The unwelcome lump in her throat had her swallowing back emotions. She wanted him to stay or at least commute back and forth.

She knew come the first of the year, she wouldn't be ready to say goodbye.

Violet put those maudlin thoughts aside and headed to the first floor. She had a job to get back to, and she planned on keeping her spirits up because there was so much good happening now. She couldn't let the future ruin her present.

Chapter Sixteen

I have OCD: Obsessive Christmas Disorder.
* Violet Calhoun

"What can I do to help?"

Violet stood in the middle of her store and glanced around. Her mother remained in the doorway separating the store from the back room. After hours was the only time to really do all the hard work. With the chocolate walk tomorrow, she wanted everything to be perfect for the customers who would be milling about down Magnolia Lane at all the businesses participating.

Simone's bakery was supplying many treats and pastries for various shops, while other shops were making their own. This was just another fundraiser for the new children's park. Tickets went on sale back in September and it was always a sellout. Plus, this kicked off the holiday shopping season in Peach Grove.

The sun had already set and her mother had offered to swing by and help, but Violet wasn't even sure where to start.

"You know your store looks lovely just like it always does," her mom said.

Violet smiled. "That's nice of you to say, but I want my

store to look fresh when my customers come in. Plus, I want to move the coffee bar a little and set up a really nice display of Simone's goodies. I have some gold-trimmed glass plates and some little lanterns to set around."

Lori stepped into the store area and moved to the coffee bar. "Are you thinking all of this up toward the nook by the front door?"

Violet stared at the space that currently housed a display of alpine snow trees and baskets with ornament groupings. "That's not where I was thinking, but I like that idea better. Are you sure you have nothing better to do on a Friday night?"

"Porter went to visit his mom at the retirement center and I told him I'd be helping you anyway. Just tell me what you want me to do."

The bell on the back door echoed through the front of the shop and Violet turned toward the doorway. Who would be stopping by at this hour and in the back door? Simone and Robin were both in their own stores working like madwomen to get ready for the rush in the morning.

When Brady stepped through, Violet smiled. "I didn't know you were stopping by. What are you doing out?"

"I had to take Luna to the vet," he told her.

Violet's smile vanished as she stepped toward him. "What happened? Is she okay?"

Brady nodded. "I wasn't paying attention and she ate something. She started choking, scared the hell out of me, so I called that emergency number. Anyway, I dropped her off and they x-rayed her. They want to watch her overnight."

"Oh, no. I'm so sorry." Violet placed a hand on his arm. "Are you okay?"

"I'm okay. The vet promised to call me if anything at

all happened, but she thought Luna would be just fine. I just feel bad for turning my back on her and missing something that was on the floor."

"I'm sorry to interrupt."

Violet jerked around, totally forgetting her mother was there. "Oh, Mom. I'm sorry. This is Brady Jackson. Brady, this is my mother, Lori Calhoun."

Brady took a step forward and extended his hand. "Pleased to meet you, ma'am. I've heard a great deal about you."

Lori's eyes went from Violet to Brady as she shook his hand. "It's a pleasure to officially meet William's grandson. I'm sorry about your loss."

Brady nodded and stepped back, sliding his hands in the pockets of his jeans. "Thank you. I didn't mean to interrupt. I just stopped on my way home from the vet when I saw Violet's Jeep out back and the lights on down here."

"You didn't interrupt a thing," her mom said with a smile. "But, who's Luna?"

"Brady's dog," Violet said.

Brady shook his head. "She's not mine. I'm just watching her for a while."

Violet rolled her eyes. "She's his."

Lori's eyes went back and forth, clearly trying to keep up and figure out what was going on.

"I can go," Brady offered. "I just wanted to let you know what was going on."

"Stay," Lori chimed in. "You're just in time to help Violet if you're free. She's getting all set up for the chocolate walk tomorrow."

Violet glanced to her mother, who was already moving toward the back.

"You don't want to stay?" Vi asked.

"I just remembered I told Porter I'd meet him for a drink."

"Mom, you said Porter was—"

"I'll see you tomorrow," her mother sang as she made haste to get out the back door.

Once they were alone, Violet laughed and looked at Brady. "Sorry about that," she said. "I guess she was trying to leave us alone."

Brady raked a hand over his normally groomed hair. The finger marks through the dark strands only proved just how stressed he'd been about Luna.

"She'll be all right," Violet assured him. "Dr. Lacy is awesome and she doesn't give false hope. She's honest. Do you know what Luna ate?"

"I was cleaning out the medicine cabinet and apparently I dropped a tube of ointment. I found a piece of the lid and a sliver of the label, but not enough to be able to tell what exactly it was."

Violet reached for him again, flattening her hand on his chest as she peered up at him. "She will be fine and we'll go down there first thing in the morning." She cringed. "Shoot. I have to be here early."

His hand came up to cover hers. "It's okay. I can go. I'm sure it's not a big deal, I've just never had anything depend on me before so it's a little nerve-racking."

Violet didn't even think before she wrapped her arms around him and pulled him close. The second she enveloped him, she wondered if she'd overstepped the boundaries...not that they'd set any. After a moment, Brady's arms came around her. His hands flattened against her back as he held her.

She couldn't help but inhale his refreshing, masculine

scent and relish in the strength of his embrace. His hands roamed up her back.

And that's when she realized that the comforting had shifted. Brady eased back just enough to gaze down, his warm breath fell on her cheek, and Violet closed her eyes. Anticipation pumped through her, but she wanted Brady to make a move…she needed him to make a move.

"I wasn't looking for this," he murmured as he grazed his stubbled jaw along hers. "I didn't want more with you."

Violet sighed. "I know you didn't. Do you want me to apologize?"

His soft chuckle vibrated against her chest. The agonizing friction from his body against hers was building her arousal, giving her a renewed sense of want and need that she hadn't felt in a long time.

Brady shifted, his eyes darting to her lips. "That's not what I want."

Violet slid her fingers along his neck and up into his hair. "What is it that you want?"

A low, guttural moan escaped him a second before his lips descended onto hers. Violet curled her fingers through his hair and opened for him. Brady's hands trailed down her back, gripped her hips and pulled her even closer.

The few stolen kisses and flirting they'd shared had all been stepping stones to this moment, but nothing could've prepared her for the passion that ignited within her. She didn't expect Brady to be so…commanding, though she should've known with his strong-willed personality.

But she didn't want to be a fling and she didn't want one night. Even though he was only here for a short time, she already felt a connection and she needed to know she wouldn't be a regret come morning.

"Are you sure about this?" she muttered against his lips.

Brady nipped at her mouth. "Positive. You?"

Honestly, right now she didn't care if he wanted just one night. She couldn't think ahead and she couldn't already be worrying about regrets. They were adults, they both wanted the same thing. All she had to do was take what she wanted.

"Yes," she told him, arching her body against his. "Yes."

She'd barely gotten the second word out when Brady cupped her backside and lifted her. He turned and started toward the back room. Violet held on, finding his strength so sexy. Everything about this man, who once irked her, she wanted to devour. She wanted him more than she remembered wanting another.

"We need to lock this back door," she told him.

Brady continued to hold on to her as he went to the door. Violet fumbled with the lock and finally slid the dead bolt in place. She hadn't realized she was so nervous, so shaky until now. Maybe it was adrenaline, maybe it was arousal.

Brady eased her down his body until her feet hit the floor. His hands came up on either side of her face, trapping her firmly between his hard body and the steel door.

Violet curled her hand around the waistband of his jeans, her knuckles grazing his lower abdomen. He sucked in a breath and his lids fluttered down. Good to know he was just as achy as she was.

With quick work, they helped each other shed their

clothes. Violet couldn't help but laugh as the moment went from intense to hurried.

"I've never gotten naked in my storage room before," she admitted.

Brady gave a half grin. "Glad to know I'm your first."

He pulled out a condom from his jeans and covered himself. Violet didn't want to ask if he was always prepared when he was around her. She was just glad he had thought of the protection.

Once again she found herself pressed against the door and lifted in his embrace. Instinctively, Violet wrapped her legs around his waist, locking her ankles at his back.

Brady smoothed her hair from her face as he stared into her eyes. Those dark eyes of his seemed almost black with arousal. The heavy-lidded gaze full of passion had knots of anticipation spiraling through her. The way he looked at her, as if waiting for her go-ahead or for her to take the lead only proved he cared, that this wasn't a fling.

Something she'd definitely have to think about later.

Violet jerked her hips against his, silently pleading for him to go ahead.

And then finally, finally, Brady joined their bodies. Violet's breath caught in her throat as her entire body tightened. She tipped her head back, curving her body to his and closing her eyes as she wanted to take in each and every sensation racking her body.

Brady jerked his hips as he held on to hers. His lips found the column of her throat and Violet gripped his shoulders as she matched his pace. His lips continued to travel over her heated skin until they found their way to her mouth. She wanted to utterly consume every part of him, she didn't want this moment to end, but her body was climbing and it had been much too long since she'd felt this way.

As her body peaked, Violet's knees pressed into Brady's sides. He murmured something about letting go and that's all she needed to completely give in to the desire and the passion.

Brady jerked harder, faster, until his entire body tightened and stilled. Violet held on, wanting to feel all of his abandonment.

Once their bodies ceased trembling, Violet pulled in a deep breath and relaxed against the door. Brady rested his forehead against hers and carefully released her legs. He continued to help hold her up with the weight of his strong body which was a good thing because she wasn't so sure her knees were ready to lock in place.

She still quavered in the aftermath, but she wasn't ready to let go quite yet.

"I don't think that was the kind of help your mother meant," Brady joked, breaking the silence.

Violet smiled and blinked, trying to focus on forming a sentence. "No, I don't imagine so."

Brady held on to her waist as he took a step back. "I can stay, though. I'm more than happy to help you do whatever you need."

The awkwardness she hadn't thought about or expected settled in. It wasn't often she stood naked and discussed her work with a man. Her eyes darted around the room, trying to take stock of where all her clothes had ended up in their haste to get undressed.

Brady must've picked up on her unease. He gathered her clothes and handed them to her before he got his own. Once she was covered, she felt marginally better. Which was silly, really, considering she'd just had fast, frantic sex against the door of her store. Now she opted to be shy?

Brady fastened his jeans and pulled his T-shirt over his head and turned to her.

"Better?"

Violet smiled. "I don't know why I'm being so goofy right now. I'm not used to this."

Brady took a step toward her. "This being sex in your back room or sex with a man you've only really known a short time?"

She shrugged. "Both."

"Regrets?" he asked, reaching up to push her hair behind her ears. His fingertips trailed down her jawline and she couldn't suppress the shiver. He seemed to be having quite the effect on her lately.

She stared up at him and smiled because she couldn't help herself. He made her feel so much, even though she wasn't ready and she certainly hadn't been expecting this.

"Not one," she told him honestly. "I guess I don't know what the protocol is now."

"There isn't any," he stated. "We get your store ready. That will help you and it will keep my mind off Luna."

Luna. Right. Comforting the pup was what started this whole thing.

No, that was wrong. That hug was what had given them that final push over the edge. They'd been leading up to this moment since…well, probably since they met.

Violet pushed aside all thoughts because right now she was running behind. But getting sidetracked had been so worth it.

"Okay, then." She couldn't help but smack her lips to his for a brief kiss. "Let's put you to work."

Chapter Seventeen

*I can't wait to sit under my tree and eat candy
out of socks.*
* Violet Calhoun

After Brady checked on Luna, and was more than re-
lieved she was going to be fine, he decided to check out
the chocolate walk since the vet told him to come by
around one to pick up the dog.

He hadn't planned on coming to the chocolate walk.
Doing things in town and getting too involved with the
community wasn't exactly what he'd had in mind. But,
after last night, everything seemed to change. Or perhaps
things changed before that.

Brady wasn't quite sure when everything turned for
him, but he was thinking less and less about Atlanta and
more and more about Violet. How was that even possible? He wanted to be back in his office, back with clients, working in a job that was hopefully going to give
him a promotion soon.

He had no clue how all of this was ever going to work
without someone getting hurt. The last thing he wanted
to do was make Violet feel like she wasn't important in
his life. With each day that passed, and especially after

last night, she was more important than he ever wanted to admit.

Brady parked the beat-up truck a block away from the main area of the chocolate walk. There were people and cars everywhere. He hadn't realized how big this event was. There was no way he could imagine how many people would show up for the Tinsel Tour.

As he walked down the street, he passed people who smiled at him. Some he recognized, some he didn't. There were families with some very excited children, some couples holding hands, a few ladies out for what was probably a girls' day. And then there was him who was a lone man walking around.

When he hit the beginning of the block that started the chocolate walk, he was greeted by a committee member at a booth. She gave him tickets for raffles at each store, a map of all the stores participating, and a shopping bag to put all of his things in.

He thanked the elderly lady and started off toward the shops. He wanted to go straight to Violet's store, but he knew she was busy.

After he'd helped her set everything up last night, he'd walked her up to her apartment over the shop, kissed her goodnight, and gone back home. He'd crawled into bed a little after two in the morning and then was back up by seven, calling to check on Luna. He wanted to see Violet, wanted to make sure she was still good after everything that had happened last night.

He wasn't sorry. He had no regrets. In fact, he wanted to see her again in his home. He wanted to see her out on the balcony off his bedroom wearing nothing but the moonlight.

Someone bumped into Brady and he startled, pulling him from his fantasy and back to reality.

"Excuse me," he turned and said.

He smiled when he saw his old teacher, Mrs. Baker. "Good to see you again, young man," she told him.

Brady nodded. "You, too. Are you shopping or only here for the chocolate?"

"All of it," she stated. "Care to walk with me?"

Brady held out his elbow. "It would be an honor."

"Charming just like your grandfather," she said, sliding her tiny hand into the crook of his arm.

He walked slower, careful to avoid bumping into others.

"There's a rumor you're selling the plantation."

He should've known nothing would stay a secret in this town. Small-town gossip was alive and well in any city in America. Peach Grove was no different.

"I live in Atlanta," he told her. "Not much I can do with that massive home when I'm not here."

"You could live here." She glanced up at him and smiled. "Imagine how happy that would've made your grandparents, knowing the next generation of Jacksons would keep up the tradition."

Yeah, he was well aware of what his grandfather would've wanted, but Brady also believed that his grandfather would've wanted him to live his life in a manner that was best for him.

"I'm not sure I'm cut out for the family life," he told her. "That house should be owned by someone who has a family to fill it. Children in the yard, family cookouts and holidays."

"You'd be a fine young man to start a family there. I

bet there's some ladies in this town who wouldn't mind scooping you up."

Brady couldn't help but laugh. He wasn't so sure he wanted "scooped up," but he also hadn't been looking for everything he'd found with Violet, either. Yet here he was, getting closer and still wanting more. Each day that passed only brought him closer to leaving, which meant his time with Violet was also drawing to an end.

Mrs. Baker gestured toward Robin's flower shop. "Let's head in here. I need to get one of her fresh arrangements for my back porch. You could use a little something, too. Your porch is sad."

"My porch is sad?" he asked, glancing down to her.

She nodded and pursed her pink lips. "Flowers brighten up any space. Just a couple of pots of some holiday arrangement. Of course, something that size would require a truck to haul it."

Brady nearly groaned. Luckily, he still had a truck right now.

"Let's go see what she's got," he stated. "I'll let you help me choose something."

When they stepped inside, Brady was stunned at the beauty inside and how Robin had taken the old building and kept all of the interior brick exposed. There was a white wash covering some of it. Large potted plants already made up sat around the perimeter. The entire middle section had a large variety of holiday arrangements and everyday bouquets. There was greenery draped around the ceiling with exposed beams from which black industrial lighting was suspended.

The place was cool as hell and Brady was seriously impressed.

There was a chocolate station set up in the back and

that's where most of the customers were. Brady wasn't necessarily interested in that, but he did like some of the larger pots.

"See anything you like?" Mrs. Baker asked.

"I do. You had a good idea."

She gave him a wink. "I'm full of them. I'm just going to look around a bit."

When he was left alone, he scoured the store for Robin. He spotted her with a customer and just decided to hang out and wait. He hadn't really talked to Violet's friends since coming into town. For some reason, he wanted to get to know that extension of her. He wanted to know everything about Vi. Although he wasn't so sure about chatting with Simone. They didn't exactly get along.

Once the customer walked away, Brady approached Robin.

"Do you have a minute?" he asked.

Robin spun around and offered a wide smile. She had her hair pulled back in a ponytail and a T-shirt with jeans and a white apron with little stripes and flowers all over it. She was a natural beauty, but she didn't compare to Violet.

He was wondering if anyone did.

"Brady, of course," she exclaimed. "It's great to see you."

"I wasn't sure you'd know who I was," he told her. "I was a bit older than you in school."

"Oh, I know who you are." She laughed. "Violet has told us about you."

He wasn't sure if that was a good or bad thing, but he wasn't about to ask.

"Uh, I think I need a couple of the large holiday pots, but I'm not sure what all Vi has planned for my house."

Now he felt ridiculous, but he did want to support all the businesses and especially Violet's friends. "Maybe I could pay for two and then you could ask her which ones would work best?"

Robin tipped her head and wrinkled her nose as her smile widened. "That is adorable. Of course, we can do that. Vi will be thrilled that you wanted to contribute. Let's get you rung up."

Brady headed to the register to pay and spotted a green and white arrangement inside a gold and white star pot. Something about it called to him and he couldn't help himself.

"Can I get this, too?" he asked, pointing to the arrangement. "And can you deliver?"

"Absolutely," Robin said and then shot him a wink. "Do I know who it's going to?"

Brady laughed. "You do. Just send it when all of this is over. I imagine she'll need something to brighten her day after all of the stress."

Robin tapped on her screen and gave him a total before she leaned forward and spoke under her breath. "I hope I'm not butting in, but are you two…you know, seeing each other?"

Brady wasn't quite sure how to answer that one. He had no clue what Violet had said and he certainly didn't want to betray the bond they shared.

"We're spending a good bit of time together," he answered honestly. "Between getting ready for the tour and her helping me with a stray dog I found, I guess you could say we're seeing each other."

He handed over his credit card. "Oh, can you keep that on file? Ring up whatever Mrs. Baker is getting as well."

Robin sighed. "You're too good to be true. Just don't hurt Violet, that's all I ask."

"I don't plan to," he told her. "We both know where we stand."

"Then I trust you if she does." Robin had him sign for the purchase and handed him back his card. "You really are too sweet. Is there a long-lost cousin of yours that I don't know about?"

Brady laughed and shifted aside as another customer came up. "I'm afraid not. Thanks again for the help."

He waited for Mrs. Baker to finish up and as soon as she got to the register, she sent him a big smile. Once she had her arrangement in hand, Brady opened the door for her and assisted her outside.

"Here, let me take this to your car," he offered. "Then you can shop more without worrying about it."

"Always the gentleman. I appreciate that."

He took the purchase and she walked beside him toward her car.

"I appreciate that gesture back there," she told him. "That was very sweet."

"Considering you made me the world's greatest beef and noodles, I'd say I still owe you."

She smacked his arm. "You owe me nothing. But it's been nice to spend some time with you. Are you enjoying your visit back here?"

"More than I thought I would."

"You might just stick around after all," she told him, pointing across the street. "That's me. The silver car."

He remembered and once he had her flowers in the back seat, he met back up with her and off they went. He found that he was having a great time going from shop to shop, filling his bag and hers. There was a line out the door to get into Violet's Christmas shop. He was so proud of her. She was doing what she loved and he knew at the end of the day, she might be tired, but she would still be smiling and loving her life.

Could he say the same? At the end of the day when he left the office was he smiling? Did he think back about how much he enjoyed his day or was he glad to be done?

"That little shop of hers is so popular," Mrs. Baker commented, pulling him back. "I'll come back later when she's not so busy. If that's okay with you?"

"Fine," he told her. "Where else would you like to go?"

"I love Mad Batter, but I just purchased some cakes yesterday for a dinner party tomorrow," she told him, glancing around the street. "I think I'd like to visit the café and maybe grab a salad to go, but that's near my car so I'll just let you go."

"I can go get your salad," he offered. "Tell me what you want and I'll deliver it to your car. How about that?"

She curled her hand through the crook in his arm once again and he led her through the crowd and toward her car. Once he had her food and told her goodbye, Brady checked his phone and it was time to go pick up Luna. He found that he wished he had more time because he was having fun. What he originally was using as a way to just pass time had become a memory he would actually cherish.

When had he become so soft? When had community gatherings and charming elderly ladies become the best things in his life?

He couldn't help but think of his grandfather. Brady knew William Jackson would love seeing his grandson enjoying the town's festivities. He would love knowing

Brady was cooperating with Violet and joining in with the Tinsel Tour.

But that guilt continued to gnaw at him regarding the sale. What other option did he have, though? He couldn't exactly commute to Atlanta each day. He didn't need a place that big when he lived alone. Well, now he had Luna, but the place was still too large for a man and a dog.

There was a family out there somewhere that would start a new chapter and a new generation. That's what the home deserved. Love and care and laughter and all the memories that a new family could make.

Brady got into the old beat-up truck. He was even at the point this ugly beast didn't piss him off so much, but he did want his car back. Something about this town was getting to him.

Or should he say…someone.

Chapter Eighteen

Oh Christmas tree, oh Christmas tree,
My skinny jeans are history.
* Violet Calhoun

The store was empty. And by empty, Violet meant the people were gone and her inventory was nearly wiped out. This was such a good problem to have.

Violet had sent an exhausted Carly home and closed up the shop. She hadn't gotten a lunch break and now it was well past six. She was going to have to go upstairs and pop something in the microwave and pull up her laptop to check the sold-out items and make sure she reordered. Everything would be here at the end of the week. She did have some back stock, but she definitely needed to reorder and probably get some new things to keep the displays fresh. Considering they were in mid-November, they still had several weeks before they actually hit Christmas.

Those weeks would fly by like they always did, but this year she wished time would go a bit slower. After New Year's, Brady would be gone.

She hadn't had a chance to speak to him since he left her at her door last night with a kiss. She'd been so busy today, she hadn't even had time to miss him or give him more than a quick thought.

But now she was alone and he was definitely at the forefront of her mind.

Violet pulled her cell from her pocket and opened the text he'd sent her several hours ago. She couldn't help but laugh at the selfie with Brady and Luna. Brady's crooked grin and Luna's mouth open like she was getting ready to attack.

Maybe it was juvenile and silly, but Violet couldn't help but make the image her lock screen. She didn't need to justify her reasoning, even to herself, but the photo made her happy and that was all she wanted out of life.

Her back door chime sounded and Violet couldn't help but wonder if that was Brady, but she figured he wouldn't leave Luna right now.

When Robin stepped through the door with a beautiful arrangement in hand, Violet smiled.

"We did it," Vi said. "This might have been the biggest chocolate walk yet. Have you talked to Simone?"

Robin shook her head. "Not yet. I just closed up and cleaned and I'm delivering this."

Surprised, Violet took a step forward and stared at the greenery and gold. "That's beautiful. Who are you delivering this to?"

"You, silly." Robin set the display on the checkout counter. "Your man came into the shop today. He ordered some pots for his porch, which you are supposed to pick out, by the way. He also bought this and asked that I bring it to you to put a smile on your face at the end of the day."

Violet couldn't help it, she knew she was beaming. No one had ever given her a surprise gift. And to know he had been thinking of her and wanted her to have a good day really made her heart swell with an emotion hovering somewhere well beyond like, but not quite to love. Damn it, though, she was close. So close to falling for the man who wasn't staying.

"Well, that was so sweet." Violet went to the arrangement and admired the simplicity and it wasn't lost on her that he'd chosen the one with stars. "It's so perfect."

"He's quite a charmer," Robin said. "He escorted Mrs. Baker around all day and even paid for her flowers."

Violet turned her attention toward her friend. "Is that right? Well, sounds like I'm not the only woman in Peach Grove who has a problem resisting Brady Jackson."

Robin sighed. "He's not staying, Vi."

Violet nodded, swallowing the unwanted emotions in her throat. "I know. I can't help but hope he might change his mind, but in my heart I know he's a city guy."

"His whole life is there," Robin agreed. "I just don't want you hurt. I know you like him, I can see it. It's apparent he's into you, too. I just worry how all this will end."

Violet worried about that very same thing, but she couldn't dwell on the unknown.

The unknown? No, that's not what this was. She knew very well how this would end. But that didn't mean she couldn't appreciate Brady and enjoy their time together while he was here.

"I need to get home," Robin told her. "There's a cup of hot chocolate and a movie calling my name."

"Oh, I meant to ask, did Lauren and Bryce come by today?" Violet asked.

Robin nodded. "I saw Bryce in the store taking photos, but we didn't talk."

"I was so slammed, if they stopped in, I didn't see them."

Robin tucked her hair behind her ears and started back toward the door before she turned. "Are you going to talk to Simone about Brady?"

"I will. I mean, I know he's not her favorite person, but that was so long ago."

"She's pretty worried that you'll get hurt."

"I know she is, but I'm fine. I swear. Nobody needs to worry about me."

Robin stared another minute before she finally walked back out. Violet shifted her gaze back to the arrangement and couldn't help the new wave of happiness that assaulted her. She couldn't just go upstairs now. She wanted to see Brady, she wanted to see Luna.

For reasons she couldn't explain, she felt more at home at the plantation than she did her own apartment. Maybe that came from years of always daydreaming that one day the place would be hers. Or perhaps it stemmed from the man who was making her feel more than she ever thought possible.

Could she already be falling for him? Was love that easy? Was she even ready to think of that word?

She had no answers to those questions, but she did know she couldn't wait to see him. Violet grabbed her phone and her keys and headed out the door, setting her alarm.

She could always work on those orders later.

Brady opened the door and was greeted with the biggest smile he'd ever seen on Violet. He'd just poured a glass of merlot and he handed it over.

"Wow," she exclaimed. "Flowers and wine. I might not let you leave."

At one time that statement would've made him cringe, but now he almost felt...warm. This just didn't make any sense. He wanted to leave, he wanted to get back to his life in Atlanta, to the partnership that awaited him.

Didn't he?

"I figured you would be by," he told her, gesturing her inside. "I hope you liked the arrangement. I saw it and just thought of you."

Violet stared up at him with those wide eyes. She should look absolutely ridiculous with that damn reindeer headband, but she just looked adorable. He'd gotten used to her quirks and her over-the-top love of the holiday.

"That was really sweet," she told him, sipping her wine. "The only time I get flowers is when I get them for myself."

"I can't tell you the last time I got anyone flowers." He thought back and all he could think of was funerals, so he said nothing. "I'm glad you liked them."

Violet leaned up and kissed him on the cheek. "I love them."

The *L* word slipping from her mouth had his heart seizing just a moment. He didn't use that word, he rarely even heard that word, especially in his line of work.

But there was also an underlying sense of need. A need to know what that word felt like, a need to know if such a thing actually existed. Would he ever know? How? It wasn't like he knew what love was.

Of course he knew what love for family felt like. He adored his grandparents and he could even say he loved his father even though he hadn't seen him for months. And his mother, well, she'd passed when he'd been younger, but he loved her even though he didn't remember her.

The love for a woman? He'd never experienced that.

"Where's Luna?" she asked, glancing around.

"She fell asleep by the sofa," he told her, leading her into the front room. "I guess all the excitement from the vet did her in. The doc gave her some bread to absorb the ointment and x-rayed her belly a few times. The bits of tubing should pass with no problem."

Violet sipped her wine and followed him into the room. "That's a relief. Puppies are like kids, or so I've always heard. They just get into things in a split second."

Violet took a seat on the sofa, slid her shoes off, and curled her legs up beneath her just like she belonged here. And she did…for now anyway. She looked perfectly right holding her wine, talking about the day, the dog sleeping at her feet.

A need he didn't recognize curled through him, but Brady had to ignore it. This wasn't reality and it wasn't long term.

"So you had a successful day?" he asked, taking a seat in the chair, though he really wanted to be on the sofa with her.

"It was amazing," she told him. "My meals today consisted of popping chocolate when I could. We sold out of nearly everything and I'm exhausted. I told Robin this was probably our biggest walk yet."

"That's great news."

"I'm not so sure my jeans will agree." She laughed. "I should have worn something with an elastic waist."

"Your waist is fine," he defended. "Expanded or not, you're perfectly fine. Do you want something to eat? I'm sure I can scrounge up something in the kitchen."

"I'm fine for now, but thanks." She took another sip and offered him a smile. "I hear you had a date for the chocolate walk."

Of course that would've gotten back to her. Brady shrugged and shifted in his chair.

"Mrs. Baker is a sweet woman. She stocked up on the sales."

Violet stared at him—her smile hadn't slipped once since she stepped through his door. He'd been right earlier. She'd work her ass off all day and then still be loving her life. Did anything get this woman down? Did she have worries or fears?

"How's everything going with clearing out the study?" she asked.

"I've made some progress. There are designated piles now. Stacks of framed pictures that can be given away, then I have boxes of family pictures, and I found more boxes with letters from my grandpa to my grandma."

"Seriously?" she asked. "Did you read any?"

Brady shook his head. "I plan on it. I don't think it's invading their privacy now that they're both gone. I think it will be like revisiting them, if that makes sense."

"It makes perfect sense." She slid her feet around her and onto the floor. "Do you want help or do you want to be alone?"

Alone? No, he'd been alone enough during his life. He wanted to be with Violet as much as he could for the time he was here.

"I'd take that help," he told her. "Let me know when you're free."

"I'm free right now." She came to her feet, causing her headband to slip. She caught it and took it off. "I forgot I was even wearing that."

Brady stood, taking the headband from her. "I'd say you're exhausted and you probably just want to crash."

"I'm tired, but I'm not going home to bed," she informed him. "I'm enjoying this glass of wine, enjoying the company, and I'd love to see some old letters."

He knew he wouldn't talk her out of this and he actually wanted the company. Brady wasn't so sure he was ready to face memories without a support system.

"Let's go, then." He reached down and picked up Luna. She moaned in his arms and settled back to sleep. "I'll just set her in her kennel while we work. I'll leave the doors open so I can hear her."

Violet chuckled. "Maybe you should get a baby monitor."

"Very funny," he joked. "The house is big, but I'll hear her if she needs out to the bathroom."

Violet reached up, her hand cupping his cheek as she leaned closer. "You really aren't the Grinch, are you?"

That soft, warm touch of hers did too many things to his already mixed-up emotions.

"Did you think I was the Grinch?" he asked.

"Maybe at one time."

He couldn't help himself. Brady snaked an arm around her waist, careful of her wine as he pulled her toward his side without the sleeping dog.

"And now?" he asked.

Her eyes widened and dropped to his mouth. "Well, now I find you a little more attractive and better company than I first thought."

He covered her lips with his for the briefest, yet powerful kiss. "That's good to know since I've thought of you since I left you last night."

They hadn't talked about what happened, not that he

knew what they should discuss. But he wasn't typically a fling type of guy and he figured that wasn't her style, either.

So now what?

"I tried to think of you today," she admitted, wrinkling her nose. "I was just so slammed. And then when Robin came in with that gorgeous arrangement, I knew I had to come here. You definitely win points for that, by the way."

"Do I get a reward?"

Violet rubbed her lips across his. "Is that why you gave me flowers?"

"I gave you flowers because I can't get you off my mind."

He shouldn't have admitted such a strong emotion, but he couldn't help himself. She deserved to know the impact she had on his life and how she was driving him out of his damn mind.

"Why don't I put Luna in her kennel and then we can meet in the study?"

Violet stepped back and smiled. "See you there."

Chapter Nineteen

You know the real hero of Christmas? Elastic pants.
* Violet Calhoun

Violet sat on the floor leaning against the leather sofa in the study. The things they'd done on that couch only moments ago still had her body heated and tingling. She honestly didn't know how to compartmentalize her emotions for Brady. They were all lumped together. She couldn't stop her feelings at the like zone. They were growing stronger and more real each day.

Brady lifted a box and set it down in front of her. She didn't mind watching those bare muscles in action. Who knew he was hiding all of that behind those uncomfortable-looking suits?

"This one has the oldest date on it, so I have to assume these were the first ones he wrote."

Violet lifted the top off and pulled out a letter. She calculated the dates in her head.

"Isn't this around the time your grandmother passed away?" she asked.

Brady glanced over her shoulder to the letter she'd unfolded. "That's the day after."

Violet had a sudden surge of remorse and a twinge of guilt. "Are you sure we should be reading these?"

His eyes met hers. "If you're not comfortable, you don't have to."

She glanced down to the letter and realized this was something so beautiful, so private, and Brady wanted to share this moment with her. If he wanted support, then she was going to be the one to give it.

"No," she told him. "This is fine."

She focused back on the letter as Brady went to dive into another box. Violet curled her feet beneath her, adjusting the oversized T-shirt of Brady's she'd thrown on.

My darling,
You've been gone less than twenty-four hours and these have been the longest of my life. I know my love and memories for you will carry on until I take my last breath and join you. I hope I gave you the best life while we were married. You deserved nothing but the best and I was so blessed to call you my wife.

We had a wonderful life together and the only regret I have is that we didn't have longer. The family will be here for your memorial service in a few days. I know how much you loved family gatherings and I know you'll be here in spirit.

Until I hold you again,
W

Violet swiped the moisture from her cheek. She hadn't even realized she'd teared up at such a heartfelt letter. The love they shared was so obvious and absolutely beautiful.

"You okay?"

Brady's question had her blinking him into focus as she swiped another escaped tear.

"Yes, sorry," she told him with a smile. "I might need a box of tissues to get through all of these letters."

She refolded the note and slid it back into the box before pulling out another. Carefully unfolding it, she started to read again. She lost track of time reading letter after letter. Every now and then she and Brady would trade and share stories or memories from the notes.

"It looks like he wrote her a letter every day from the day she passed away," Brady stated hours later. "I never knew."

Violet had moved to the sofa a while back and now Brady sat on the floor in front of her. He shifted and turned to focus on her and she could have sworn his eyes were a little misty.

"They had a true romance story," Violet said. "It's not often people find love like that."

Brady glanced back down to his lap and the stack of letters he held. She wondered what was rolling through his mind, but she figured he needed to process his emotions. Violet gave him the time and space to do that and she would wait on him to say or do something.

"You know, in my line of work, I don't hear people say I love you, let alone show it." He held the letters up. "These are so rare and it's just proof marriages can and do last. I've never known any couple like my grandparents. I knew they had a strong bond, but I never realized how strong until now."

"Sometimes you just find the right person," Violet said.

He turned his attention back to her once again. "Do you believe that? Like there's a person for everybody?"

Violet shrugged. "I'm not sure. I mean, I believe in love. I've seen it with my father and his wife and my mom and Porter. We've just read about it with your grandparents. It's impossible to ignore."

"I'm starting to see that," he murmured. "I guess I never realized that was such a strong emotion. I'm always so engrossed in my job and it's extremely rare that my client ends up making amends and getting back together with their ex."

"I would imagine that atmosphere would make for a stressful workday and nothing fun would come from that."

"It's stressful," he agreed. "I never even thought about how much so until I came here on a forced vacation. And the idea of a job being fun certainly never crossed my mind. I mean, I went to law school because I wanted to help people and the money would be good. I wanted to be important."

Violet swung her legs over the side of the couch next to where he sat on the floor. Then she leaned down and grabbed his face, looking him straight in the eyes.

"You're important no matter what career you choose or how much money you make," she told him. "It doesn't matter the numbers in your bank account. My own account is laughable and I'm pretty sure I'm happier than you."

Brady smiled. "I know you're a happier person. You make people smile when you walk in a room. You made my grandfather happy and kept him busy with community projects. You're special, Vi."

That might be the most expressive she'd ever heard him about anything. And those emotions were directed toward her. She didn't know quite what to think or where to go from here. There was so much she wanted to say, and she would say everything on her mind and in her heart if she thought for a second he would stay.

But he wasn't and this relationship, for lack of a better term, had a time limit and the clock was quickly ticking down.

"What are we doing?" she asked him, releasing his face and sliding down onto the floor beside him.

"Going through old letters."

She slid her hand onto his thigh and rested her head on his shoulder. "I meant with us. I don't know what's going on or even what to think."

Silence settled between them as he laid his hand over hers. There was no way to deny the deeper bond they had just experienced…and not only the physical intimacy. There was another layer they had just added to everything else and Violet wondered if this would be enough to stand on.

Was she naïve in thinking about how a long-distance relationship would work? Should she even mention it? Granted he wasn't leaving for another six weeks, but that wasn't near long enough for her.

"I don't know," he whispered. "I don't have the answers."

Yeah, neither did she. So where did that leave them? Likely he felt the same in that he wanted more, but their separate lives didn't quite mesh together. There was no way she could ever move from Peach Grove. She loved her life here…just as he loved the life he'd created for himself in Atlanta.

Violet turned her hand over, lacing her fingers through his. "Well, I'm not in a hurry for this to stop," she told him honestly. "And I'm not going to like it when you leave."

His soft chuckle vibrated his body against hers. He shifted, kissing the top of her head and wrapping an arm around her.

"I'm not, either," he murmured as he pulled her closer. "But we don't have to think about that right now."

Right. But that didn't change the outcome, and the looming date still hovered in the distance, staring her down like the inevitable enemy.

"That sounds perfect," Violet stated. "I'll meet you there then. Thanks so much."

She hung up with the manager from the library and had arrangements in place for a very special delivery to Brady's house later this afternoon.

Violet continued working on a new display of little gnomes that looked like elves. She'd only bought a few, but they had been such a hit with customers, she'd ordered more.

After the chocolate walk last week, she'd placed a large order to restock and bring in some brand-new items. The white faux fur wreaths were absolutely stunning hanging in her windows at various lengths. She'd also intermingled strands of gold stars among the wreaths.

She glanced over to the decorative windows on either side of her front door. She'd never used gold stars in her windows before, but she loved this simple, classy look. She couldn't help but smile at the inspiration.

Everything seemed to be clicking in place. Her shop, the Tinsel Tour in less than a week, and even her life with Brady. She hadn't slept in her own apartment in nearly a week. They had some unspoken agreement that after she got off work she'd just end up at his house, where he would have a glass of wine and a meal ready for her. They'd been reading more letters, watching movies cozied up on the sofa with Luna, and going to bed together.

Violet couldn't lie to herself. She loved this temporary familial life they had. *Temporary* really was an ugly word, but she had to keep repeating it in her mind so she didn't confuse fantasy for reality.

She'd also told herself that there was nothing wrong with taking what she could get right now. It wasn't settling for less, it was enjoying the moment and the man. Maybe she would get hurt in the end, but right now she deemed the heartache worth it. She'd rather have something real with Brady for a short time, than nothing at all forever.

The front door opened and Simone popped her head in. "Is now a good time?" she asked.

Violet laughed. "Of course. Come in. What's up?"

"I've got Maureen running the place, but since she's a new hire, I don't want to be gone too long."

Simone shut the door behind her and glanced around. "Oh, new things. I'll have to come shop later when I have more time."

Violet stacked another short, fat gnome next to the tall, skinny one. "Is something wrong?"

"No. I just…well, yes." Simone sighed and came to stand near the display. "I don't want to come across as bitchy or good grief, jealous, but why haven't you talked to me about Brady?"

Violet stilled, her gaze darting from the display to her friend. "Honestly, I wasn't trying to keep anything from anybody. We were working on the tour, things kept progressing, and now…well…"

"You're staying at his house."

Violet nodded. "I have been. How did you know?"

"I just guessed. I've come by your place the past two nights to talk and you haven't been home."

"You haven't texted me," Violet said.

"I didn't want to bother you if you were at Brady's house." Simone took a step forward and reached for Violet's hand. "I just want you to be okay. That's all."

Violet knew her friend meant well. She knew her friend wasn't in any way jealous. Good heavens, she and Brady only went on a handful of dates years ago. That meant nothing. Simone was legitimately worried and Violet smiled to ease her friend's mind.

"I promise, with my whole heart, that I am fine." Violet squeezed Simone's hand. "I know he's not staying, and yes, we have gotten pretty close. All we're doing is taking things day by day. I definitely wasn't hiding from you, but to be honest, I haven't even talked to my mother about this, either."

Violet realized she'd been so busy between the tour and spending time with Brady that she hadn't really done anything with her gal pals. No wonder Simone came looking for her.

"You know we all just love and care about you," Simone added. "That's the only reason we butt into your life."

Violet smiled and pulled her friend in for a hug. "I know. I'd do the same if the tables were turned."

Simone eased back. "Well, I should get back to the shop. I don't like to leave seasonal workers alone too long."

"How are your ticket sales for the tour?" Violet asked.

"I've sold them all."

Violet smiled. "That's what I want to hear."

"Text me later." Simone moved to the door. "And I love your new window displays. They are different for you, but perfect."

Violet was still smiling after her friend walked out. Yeah, her life was much different than it had been a month ago. Everything had changed from her decorating to her outlook on life.

She absolutely couldn't wait to see Brady's face when the final piece for his theme was delivered. She couldn't recall being more excited for a home than she was for this one.

Violet decided to just live in this moment of excitement and nothing else. Brady made her happy, her work made her happy, and nothing else mattered.

Chapter Twenty

Ho, ho, ho... Pour the merlot.
* Violet Calhoun

"Stay out back with Luna, okay?"

Brady had no idea what was going on, but Violet was nearly giddy with excitement over something. He almost wondered if he should be afraid, but he trusted her...for the most part. When it came to Christmas, he really didn't know what all she was capable of.

"I promise," he told her.

Brady snapped his fingers for Luna to follow and he led her out the back door. She was getting more and more used to him and growing accustomed to the house. There were very few accidents, too. He couldn't help but love this dog and part of him was glad nobody had ever stepped forward to claim her.

Once they were outside, Brady grabbed the rubber ball and gave it a toss. They played fetch for a while until Brady's cell rang. He threw the ball once more before pulling his phone from his pocket.

"Brady Jackson."

"Brady. Is this a good time to talk?"

Frank Myers's familiar tone slid through the line, and Brady's nerves kicked in.

"This is fine," he replied. "What can I do for you?"

"Just checking in on you," Frank said. "How is life in Peach Grove? Are you able to get some work done with your grandfather's house?"

"Making some headway." Luna brought the ball back and Brady took it from her and threw it a little farther. "I've spoken with a Realtor about selling and I'm getting some things cleaned out."

"You sound good. How are you feeling?"

Brady felt like he was talking to a shrink instead of his boss, but he also knew Frank meant well and genuinely cared about his employees. "I feel great."

Luna dropped the ball in front of him and then barked when he didn't get it fast enough.

"Is that a dog?" Frank asked.

"Yes. A pup I found the other night in the park."

Frank chuckled. "Taking in a stray puppy sounds like a commitment. I never took you for a man who liked permanent things."

Yeah, he hadn't been that way until recently. What could he say, this town had changed him. Or maybe the change came from the combination of Violet, Luna, and the community. He didn't hate it here. He remembered loving this place as a child and now as an adult, he could honestly say those emotions were back, but even stronger.

"I'm not the same guy I was a month ago," he told Frank. "I feel really good."

"Better watch or I'll lose you to that town."

Even though Frank laughed, Brady didn't see the humor. Perhaps that was because he was feeling torn in different directions. On one hand was his career in the city and the other hand held his personal life in the small town. There was no way to combine the two.

Could he even trust what he was feeling now with Violet? If he gave up his career in Atlanta, and things fell through with Vi, then where would he be?

"I assume you're still looking forward to the first of the year," Frank went on. "We've done some updates to your office while you've been gone and everything should be ready when you return."

"Updates?"

"Corbin turned in his resignation," Frank told him. "His wife took a job at a hospital in Miami so he's leaving. You're going into his office. He went ahead and moved over to yours so we could paint and do a few things."

Corbin's office was in the corner with two walls of windows. Pretty much a coveted spot and now it would be waiting for Brady along with a partnership prospect.

"That's great to hear," Brady commented. "I hate to be losing Corbin, but I wouldn't turn down that office."

"Brady."

He turned toward the back patio door and saw Violet. She waved him in and had the widest smile he'd ever seen. His heart tumbled in his chest and there was a tightness he couldn't explain.

He held up a hand for her to hold on one minute.

"Frank, I need to go. Thanks for checking in."

"See you soon, Brady. And have a good Thanksgiving."

"You, too."

Brady hung up and laughed. He hadn't even thought about Thanksgiving being in a few days. He just knew the Tinsel Tour was the Saturday after Thanksgiving. It had been on that day every year since his grandfather started it.

He called for Luna as he made his way up onto the patio.

"Sorry," Violet told him. "I didn't realize you were on the phone."

"No problem. Just a work call."

Her smile dipped just a bit, but enough that he caught it. Clearly his work was a touchy topic for both of them, so best to just ignore it. He didn't want anything to dampen her good mood and ruin her surprise.

"Am I allowed back into the house now?" he asked.

Violet nodded. "Yes, but you have to follow me and when I tell you to close your eyes, you have to obey me."

"A forceful woman? I think I like this side of you."

"Because I haven't been forceful before now?" She laughed.

"Good call." Brady glanced around to make sure Luna was with him before he followed Violet inside the house. "I assume this has to do with the tour?" he asked.

"It does, but it's upstairs." She stopped at the base of the steps and glanced back at him. "I know I said everything stayed on the first floor, but I couldn't resist. You'll understand when you see."

She went up the stairs and headed down the hallway toward one of the spare bedrooms in the front of the house. Then she stopped at the closed door and turned to face him.

"Okay, close your eyes and give me your hands."

He held out his hands and did as he was told. "You're not going to take me out here and throw me over the balcony, are you?"

"Oh, hush and come on."

The door creaked open and she tugged on his hands. He carefully took a step forward, remembering the layout of this room. The bed was over to the left with a dresser and sitting chair to the right. The balcony doors were straight ahead and that was the direction they were headed.

"You are taking me to the balcony," he accused.

"Just be quiet and keep those eyes closed," she ordered. "It's almost time."

The balcony door eased open and the warm breeze washed over him. Violet released his hands and he heard her shift away.

"Okay. Open your eyes."

Brady blinked against the bright sunshine and that's when he saw it. A large telescope pointed toward the sky. This was the exact spot where he and his grandfather used to look up at the sky for hours upon hours. Brady took a step forward and glanced all over the telescope before squinting one eye and looking through the lens.

"This is amazing," he told her, turning his attention to her. "Where did you get this?"

"The library." She came to stand by him and rested her hand on the telescope. "This was your grandfather's. He'd had it several years and just donated it right before he passed."

The meaning of her words settled in. William had indeed purchased a new telescope, but Brady hadn't come back to see it. The guilt that had been there from the time William passed still settled deep, but there was a sense of something more positive that really grabbed him. Brady felt like he was getting some closure from this. Or maybe a second chance to really have a moment and a bond like he and his grandfather shared.

"You really are perfect at your job," he murmured, glancing into her eyes.

"I told you I wanted you to love this as much as I do."

He couldn't imagine anything more meaningful. "And this telescope goes along with my theme?"

Violet nodded, still smiling. "Watching for Santa is your theme. I have all the gold stars downstairs and I will decorate this bedroom since people will be walking through, but that's not a big deal. What's one more Christmas tree?"

Sure. What was one more? She'd already put up six on the first floor and she was still waiting on him to help decorate two of them.

"This is one of the coolest things," he told her. "We have to come back out tonight when the stars are out."

Violet reached for him and pressed her hand against his chest. "I was hoping for a little astronomy lesson."

He grabbed her around the waist and pulled her in. "I'll give you any lesson you want."

"Is that a promise?" she asked.

Brady dipped his head and covered her mouth. Damn, this woman could make him forget everything...including the exciting phone call with his boss. He didn't have these feelings when thinking of going back to Atlanta. Being here with Violet gave him a burst of hope and happiness he'd never felt before.

How could he ignore this? How could he ignore the strong bond they were already forming? The woman knew exactly what to do to pull emotions from him he thought were long dead and buried.

But now could he just give up his career?

Ignoring that inner battle, Brady wrapped his arms

around Violet and lifted her off her feet for a moment before setting her down and releasing her mouth.

"This is the nicest thing anyone has ever done for me," he told her. "I know it's part of the tour and I know it's only temporary, but I also know you went to some trouble to include a part of me with this."

She threaded her fingers through his hair and smiled. "I'm glad I could make you happy. That's been my goal from the beginning."

That's true. From the moment she showed up on his doorstep with that ridiculous headband on her head, she'd wanted him to love this tour and be part of it. She'd reached her goal, but had he? Hell, at this point he wasn't even sure he knew what his goal was.

"I've been meaning to talk to you about Thanksgiving," she said. "I had an idea, but if you're not comfortable with it, just say so."

"Sounds like I should be worried."

Her hands came to rest on his shoulders as she shrugged. "No need to worry, just throwing this idea out there. I typically get together with my mom, Robin, and Simone. But I was wondering if we could gather here and invite my mother and Porter."

Brady thought about the idea of a Thanksgiving meal around a table. He didn't remember the last time he had a real Thanksgiving meal. The idea of spending a day with Violet's friends and mother seemed a whole other level of deep relationship that he should run the hell away from. He should turn her down and tell her he was spending the day alone and she should go with her friends.

"That sounds nice."

How the hell did that slip out of his mouth without his

permission? But her smile widened and her brows rose as her eyes held his.

"Really?" she asked. "I was hoping you'd say yes, but I worried you'd feel like this was…well, a big step in a direction we shouldn't be going."

"No, we shouldn't," he agreed. "But I know my grandfather would've loved having this house filled with love and memories again. Plus, I haven't had a real Thanksgiving in years."

She smacked her lips to his again and then stepped back with a little squeal of excitement.

"I am going to make this the best Thanksgiving meal you've ever had," she promised. "I need to get to the store. Do you have a favorite dish or do you want to be surprised?"

"You can surprise me."

"This is great," she said. "I have to send out a group text and get started on prepping the dining room."

"Aren't you decorating for the tour?"

"I am, but the table has to be set for Thanksgiving. Seriously, just leave this up to me. I gotta run."

And then she was gone. Brady laughed at how fast her mind went from one idea to the next. He couldn't keep up and felt it best for his sanity that he not try. This dinner might be awkward with her mother and Simone, but he was quickly finding he'd do anything to make Violet happy.

He turned back to the telescope and an idea hit him hard. While she was out doing her thing, he had his own surprise to gear up for. He couldn't wait until she came back and night fell. This whole trade-off of surprising each other was starting to become a pattern, but definitely one he didn't want to stop.

Chapter Twenty-One

I'm Santa's favorite elf.
* Violet Calhoun

Violet hadn't expected to be gone for hours and return after the sun had set. And she certainly hadn't expected to spend so much, but this was her very first event to host at the home she'd always dreamed...with the man she didn't know she'd been dreaming of.

Here she was with everything she'd ever wanted. Even if for a short time, there was no way she wasn't going to go all out and make this holiday the most exciting ever. This might just top her love of Christmas...but she doubted it.

Even with the Tinsel Tour only a few days away, Violet planned to devote all of her spare time to this party. She had her volunteers still working on homes around the town and so far, so good. All of the tickets had sold out and Lauren had already texted her about going on the tour and the best times to get some good shots for Bryce.

Everything was going perfectly. Maybe a little too perfectly because always looming in the distance of her mind was the fact her little fantasy world going on now was exactly that...a fantasy.

Once she got all of the bags in the house, she walked out back to see if Brady and Luna were around. When she didn't see them, she went back inside and started calling for him. The house was so big, but his borrowed truck was still out front, so she knew he was here.

"Upstairs," Brady yelled.

Violet made her way to the second floor and heard Brady's voice as he said something to the dog. She couldn't help but get that warm feeling all through her. The man wasn't grouchy like she'd first thought. He had a hard exterior, but that inner man was soft and vulnerable and totally human.

She knew it was pointless to ignore the fact she'd fallen in love with him. Not that she would ever tell him. That was something that would really put a stumbling block between them.

When the time came for Brady to leave Peach Grove, she wanted him to leave with memories and ready to go back to the career he'd worked so hard for.

He stepped into the hallway from the spare bedroom and Violet laughed.

"Have you been out with that telescope since I left?" she asked.

Then she glanced and saw there was so much more than just the telescope on the balcony. Brady had spread a blanket over the floor and had a variety of food and wine displayed.

"Wow, you've been busy," she told him. "I'm impressed."

"I wanted to show you the stars, but then I figured you probably didn't even think of eating while you were out running errands. I hope you like sandwiches and fruit. I wasn't sure what else to have since I didn't know when you'd be back."

Violet crossed to him and gave him a kiss. "This is perfect. I love it. Where's Luna?"

"I put her up when the front door alarm went off and I knew you were home."

That she was *home*. Those words slipped out and she wasn't sure if he meant to say them or if he realized the impact that sentence had. She couldn't think of the Jackson mansion as home. She was staying here, yes, but only to be with Brady until he left. This place would sell, no doubt fast, at the first of the year.

Violet slipped her sandals off and walked onto the blanket. "Let's see what we have. I'm pretty hungry."

Brady sat down and patted the spot beside him. Vi sank down and crossed her legs. She was still really stunned that he'd thought of doing this. She knew he wanted to show her the stars, but she had no idea he would go all out like this.

"What can I make you?" he asked.

Violet reached for a sliced strawberry. "Anything at all. I'm not picky."

As he put her sandwich together, Violet pulled in a deep breath. She didn't necessarily want to broach the subject, but she felt the elephant in the room should probably be addressed.

"You're going to spoil me," she told him.

"I'd say we've spoiled each other," he countered as he handed her a napkin with her food. "I really wanted to just remain alone and in private. I wanted to box up memories and things and sell the house and be gone. I guess coming to a small town and trying to remain on the down low is impossible."

Violet laughed. "Even without me beating down your door, people would've noticed you back in town." She took the glass of wine he poured and set it down. "I just don't want this to get awkward when you leave."

He turned his attention toward her. "Is this what you want to talk about?"

"Not really," she admitted. "But don't you think we should?"

"I'd rather ignore the fact that I'm leaving and just spend my time with you."

If he wanted to ignore it, then didn't that mean he didn't want to leave? If he was unsure, why didn't he just stay until they could see what happened between them?

She had so many questions, but he'd just stated he didn't want to talk about the topic, so she wasn't about to start an unnecessary argument. "Then we should just focus on Thanksgiving, the Tinsel Tour, and then the greatest holiday of all."

Brady laughed. "Do you even get sleep during this time of year? Because you go to bed late, you wake early, and you're always on the go."

"I do get less sleep. My mind is always going in a million directions and I just want to make the holidays great for the whole town. I live for this every year."

"That's why everything is such a success," he told her. "This town is lucky to have you and your friends working on these projects. It's when people care about their work that it really shows."

"Thank you. That's quite a compliment. It's definitely more pressure this year with *Simply Southern* here, the fiftieth anniversary, and the first year without William. I just need everything to be perfect."

"It will be," he assured her.

Once they finished their little picnic, Brady took all the dishes inside and then came back out. He stood at the telescope and looked through the lens. After a few adjustments, he must have found the sight he wanted.

"Okay," he said. "Come here and look at this constellation."

Violet looked through the scope and was shocked at the brightest, clearest stars in a formation.

"That is beautiful," she said, glancing back to Brady. "What's this one called?"

"Cassiopeia. She was a boastful queen and it's said that six months out of the year, this constellation is upside down in the sky as her punishment for being so vain."

"Wow." Violet went back to looking through the lens. "That's a bit harsh. It's just so beautiful, though. Show me more."

She stepped aside and watched as Brady adjusted again and found more for her to see. He showed her many stars, told her their names, explained how the stars she was seeing now were actually billions of years old. Violet had no idea stars were so complex and interesting.

"No wonder you were so fascinated," she told him. "This is really cool. And it makes you even hotter when you explain all of this with those dark glasses on. Like a sexy professor."

Brady reached up and slid her curls behind her ears, his fingertips trailed down her jawline.

"Is that right?" he asked. "Had I known you liked these glasses so much, I would've worn them more often."

"Maybe you can wear those now…only those," she suggested. "And the moonlight. Oh, and maybe a smile."

He chuckled and pulled at the hem of his shirt, easily stripping it off and tossing it aside. "If we're about to have sex on my balcony at night, then hell yes, I'll be wearing a smile."

Violet started stripping from her clothes, too. They were laughing and flinging clothes and tumbling down to the blanket.

Brady lay on his back, pulling Violet on top of him to straddle his lap. Staring down at him, she realized she had completely fallen for him. If she hadn't realized it before now, this would have definitely put her over the edge.

"You look beautiful," he murmured as he grazed his hands up her bare thighs. "Just like this, wearing nothing but the moonlight. I knew this would be a good idea."

She rested her palms flat on his chest. "So you had this planned all along? Seducing me with your intelligence?"

"It worked, didn't it?"

Violet leaned down, moving her hands to either side of his face as her hair curtained them. "Oh, it definitely worked."

Violet joined their bodies, her eyes totally locked on Brady. His eyes closed as he arched, his fingertips digging into her hips. Seeing him completely exposed, both physically and emotionally, was something she never tired of. Knowing she had broken through that tough exterior in such a short time had her wondering if he'd ever made a connection like this with another.

But she pushed aside all thoughts, not wanting anything to come between them now. There was nothing more important than Brady and the short time they had to spend with each other.

She leaned down, covering his mouth with hers as he gripped her backside and started jerking faster. She broke the kiss, now resting her forehead against his as her breath came out in heavy pants. Her entire body climbed and the euphoric climax slammed into her.

Brady let out a low moan—his hold on her tightened as his body stilled beneath hers. Violet shifted, letting her head fall to that crook in his neck as her body slowly came down, but still very much tingled from head to toe.

Moments later, Brady's fingertips trailed up her back, giving her even more shivers. Then he grabbed hold of the comforter and wrapped it around them.

"I've got to be killing your back," she told him, starting to slide to the side.

He caught her, holding her steady and pulling the blanket tighter.

"Don't move," he murmured. "I love the feel of your weight on me. You do something to me, Vi. I can't explain it, but I don't want to leave this moment. So just... stay right here."

Violet nestled deeper into that perfect spot between his neck and his shoulder. How could she argue with his logic? There wasn't anywhere else she wanted to be. If this night could last forever, she'd be so happy.

But Violet knew this memory would last her a lifetime. She would never forget every single day she spent with Brady and the perfect bond they'd formed.

Violet stood back and stared at the table. It wasn't her favorite table setting, but with only two days to get that and a large dinner together, Violet was pretty proud of what she'd accomplished.

The doorbell rang and she started to go get it, but Brady called out that he had it. Violet went back into the kitchen to check the turkey. Thankfully she'd found a caterer who was selling pre-cooked turkeys and all Violet had to do was heat this one up for the time and temperature she was told. This dinner had definitely been a joint effort because she was absolutely awful in the kitchen. She'd read the recipe for dressing balls and decided those sounded easy enough. She also tried her hand at a corn casserole. Everything else she doled out for others to bring. Thankfully her best friend owned a bakery, so if nothing else, they would at least have some amazing desserts.

She heard her mother's voice a minute before her mom stepped through the kitchen doorway.

"There's my girl," her mother said with a wide smile. "Happy Thanksgiving."

"Happy Thanksgiving, Mama. Is Porter with you?"

"He's talking to Brady," she confirmed. "Here are the mashed potatoes as requested with an extra dollop of cream cheese."

"Perfect. You always made the best." Violet pointed to the island. "Set them over there. I think we'll do a buffet style and keep all the food in here."

"Is that because you've set the table and you don't want anyone messing up your decorations?"

"That's exactly why," Violet laughed.

An echo of voices sounded down the hall and moments later, Simone and Robin stepped through holding their dishes.

"Happy Thanksgiving, everyone," Simone exclaimed. "I brought a little of everything so I hope everyone is happy."

"I've got the hash brown casserole and the green beans." Robin set her carrier down on the island. "Is there anything I can do to help?"

Violet glanced around and shook her head. "I don't

think so. The turkey is ready to be carved. We can just spread the food out here. Sims, you can take your desserts to the buffet in the dining room."

Violet put on her pot holders and pulled the turkey from the oven. It looked like it might actually be fine. Fingers crossed.

"Lori." Porter came into the kitchen with Brady and stepped up to the island where everyone had gathered. "Did you know Brady is selling this place?"

Violet met her mother's eyes across the kitchen for a brief moment before Lori turned her attention to Porter.

"I didn't know that," she told him. "Are you looking to buy us a new place?"

Porter laughed. He crossed the kitchen to stand next to Lori. He slid his arm around her waist and kissed the side of her head. The man absolutely was perfect for her mom. The light in his eyes when he looked at her couldn't be dimmed or hidden.

"If this is what you want," he told her. "You know I'd do anything for you."

Violet glanced to Brady. "Do you want to carve the turkey?"

He looked like she'd just asked him to fly to the moon.

"I've never carved a turkey," he murmured.

"Well, might as well try now," she told him. "I don't think you can mess this up."

She pulled out the carving knife and handed it over. Everyone else started filling their plates and Brady passed over turkey slices as he carved. There was a sense of calmness, nothing awkward or uncomfortable now that they were all here together.

Perhaps because this was Thanksgiving, perhaps because her friends and her mother knew Violet was living in the moment and just enjoying herself.

After they were all seated at the table—Brady ended up on the side and Violet landed at the head—chatter started once again about the sale of the home.

"Violet offered to stage the home and throw an open house after the tour," Brady told them. "I'm due back in Atlanta on January 2nd so I hope to at least have an offer or be under contract before I go."

Violet concentrated on eating and not the doom and gloom this conversation had turned to. Reality really sucked sometimes. She liked the world she made up of magical Christmas homes and putting smiles on people's faces with her events…which was exactly what she'd be doing once Brady left. Her life would go on just like his pass-through didn't happen.

Yet getting close with Brady, learning more about William and his love story, had changed everything within her. She would definitely come out the other side a completely different woman.

"That's going to be a fun open house," Lori said. "Vi, I bet you're thrilled to stage this home."

Violet nodded. "I'm excited for the tour and the staging. So many things going on right now."

"She's the busiest person I've ever met," Brady stated. "And that's saying something since I'm married to my job."

Simone laughed. "I can attest to that."

Violet watched as Simone and Brady stared at each other, then shared a laugh.

"Good to see you after all these years," he told her. "I see you're skipping the turkey."

"I'll stick with veggies and carbs, thanks."

"So," Robin interjected. "Brady, are you listing with an agent?"

"I don't think so. I want Violet to do her event and I know it will not have a problem selling. Plus, I'm not worried about the legal side of the sale."

Porter reached for his glass of sweet tea. "We're going to be needing a new prosecutor come next election. Be mighty grand if a Jackson still lived in town and wanted to run."

Violet's food nearly caught in her throat. She hoped she covered up her half choking by grabbing her drink and pushing the lump of emotions down. Porter throwing that bomb out there wasn't something she had expected. She glanced over to Brady and saw that he seemed just as caught off guard.

"I'm a divorce attorney," he told Porter. "I did work in a criminal law office when I first graduated law school, though."

Porter shrugged. "Just throwing that out there. Something to think about. Or, you can stay in Atlanta and I'll consider buying this place. It's the most coveted home in all of Peach Grove. I know because my office has gotten calls about it. Some of the elders in the town have asked if this will be turned into a museum to showcase the history of the town."

"A museum?" Violet asked. "This can't be a museum. A family needs to be here. Children should be running in the yard, family reunions need to happen on nice spring days, the house needs to stay on the Tinsel Tour."

"And don't forget the dog," Brady added with a smile. "You had said this house requires a dog, too."

"Speaking of, where is Luna?" Violet's mother asked.

"I put her in her kennel while we're eating," Brady

said. "She's getting bigger and a little bolder, thinking I won't punish her."

"That's because you don't punish her," Violet added. "She's got you completely wrapped around her little paws."

As the conversation shifted from Brady's move to the potential political position to dogs, Violet took a moment and just let everything settle in. All the what-ifs started flooding her mind.

What if Brady stayed?

What if Brady went back to work, but didn't sell the house?

What if he decided that taking a chance on her and on Peach Grove was the right move?

Only time would tell, but she did know one thing. She wasn't about to ask him to stay. He had to make his own decisions and be happy with the life he chose.

Chapter Twenty-Two

*May you never be too grown-up to search
the skies on Christmas Eve.*
* Violet Calhoun

Brady couldn't believe the whirlwind named Violet that swept through his home and transformed it into some type of Christmas wonderland. The large sign in the yard showcased the theme and she didn't leave anything out. His entire first floor sparkled with gold stars, there was garland of gold sleds draped up the banister and across the mantels of all the fireplaces.

In the bedroom leading to the balcony and telescope, she'd put a teddy bear on the bed and made it resemble a child's bedroom. Seeing that display hit him hard. He hadn't expected decorations to have such an impact, but they did.

This house should have a family, like Violet kept saying. The fact there were people who thought of turning this into a museum didn't sit well with him. He'd definitely be choosy about who he sold to.

He also wanted this home to remain on the Tinsel Tour. Not that he could make that a stipulation, but surely if a local bought the home, like Porter, they would keep the plantation in the rotation. That was so important to Violet and he wanted to do everything he could to make her happy.

Brady had no clue how she pulled all of this off, still made time for him, ran her store, and came out with a smile on her face like she wasn't the least bit tired.

Violet had asked him to stay home and help with his home on the tour. She would be going from house to house with Lauren and Bryce, explaining the tour and giving the history of the homes.

This was her day to shine and he had no doubt she'd excel. He wished he could follow her around and see her in her element, but she would get here soon enough.

Simone had provided each home with treats for the community on their walk. There were carriage rides taking people from house to house who couldn't walk for a disability or their age. Throughout the town there were also hot chocolate and hot cider stations set up.

The woman literally thought of everything.

Brady made sure Luna had gone out to potty before he put her with a new bone in her kennel. He came downstairs just in time for the first round of walkers. He didn't see Violet, yet. With each tour group that came through was a guide to explain the home and the themes.

Brady recognized a few people who passed through his door. Clearly more people knew him than he recalled because several people told him how wonderful it was to have him in town. He was hugged, he was told stories of his grandparents, he was asked multiple times if he was staying in town.

By the time Violet came through with the magazine crew, he was so thankful to have her here now.

She had on a green sweater and jeans with little booties. She'd left her hair down and curled and had put on her reindeer headband that he'd seen her in that first day.

Of course he'd seen her before she left, but this seemed different. Now she was all on with this. For the moment she'd planned and prepared for over the past year. He knew she'd started working on this with his grandfather and then after William passed, she had taken over the whole thing. Just like the amazing woman he'd come to know and…

Love?

Did he love her? What the hell did he know about love?

"Isn't that right, Brady?"

He blinked, focusing on Violet, who stood in the entryway with Bryce and Lauren. Bryce was snapping photos of the stairwell and Lauren and Violet seemed to be waiting on Brady to answer.

"I'm sorry, what?" he asked.

Violet blinked, staring at him. "Everything all right?"

He nodded. "Yes, just let my mind wander for a minute. What were you saying?"

"I was telling Lauren that your grandparents started this tour fifty years ago and this home has been in your family since it was built nearly two hundred years ago."

"That's right," he said, turning his attention to the journalist. "When my grandfather passed, he willed the plantation to me. I spent every summer here growing up."

"Peach Grove is a gorgeous little town," Lauren said, taking notes. "I'm tempted to move here. It's like something out of a movie. Is it always this cozy and friendly?"

Violet laughed. "Pretty much. Of course we have some small-town drama like any other place, but for the most part, people always come together for community events. Robin, Simone, and I make up the community events committee and we're always making sure there is something going on or something to look forward to."

"She's really amazing at her job," Brady added. "My grandfather would be so proud of the work she's continuing to do."

Bryce came back over. "I'd like to get a photo of the two of you on the porch, if that's okay."

Brady glanced to Violet who nodded. "Fine by me," she said.

He didn't necessarily want to be in any photos. By the time the magazine came out, the house would already be on the market and him posing as the owner seemed like a lie.

But he followed Violet out onto the porch. They followed Bryce's instructions on where to stand and how to pose. Violet stood by the post with her arm around it slightly while Brady sat casually on the top porch step. He took another with Brady in the same position and Violet stood at the opening of the door like she was welcoming a guest inside.

"That should do it here," Bryce announced. "We ready to move on?"

"Let's go," Lauren said, then turned to Brady. "Thank you for showing us your lovely home. This really is quite a beautiful tradition your grandparents started. You should be really proud."

Guilt niggled at him, knowing that this wasn't a tradition he would be involved in again.

"I am proud of what they did for this town," he replied.

Violet turned away and started down the steps. Likely she wasn't too keen on the future, either, but this was the reality. This was what he came here to do and he had to see his plans through so he could get back to his real life.

All of this was temporary, almost a fantasy life he'd been living. He was sent here to relax and he'd far exceeded what he thought.

Once the magazine crew and Violet were gone, Brady continued to talk to guests as they came through. Many people were excited about the telescope up on the second-story porch. He made sure to mention that Violet had come up with that idea and the library had graciously donated the telescope for the tour.

By the time the night came to an end, Brady was exhausted. The treats were all gone, the house was quiet, and he wasn't sure when Violet would return.

He went upstairs to get Luna and took her out back to run around and do her business. The more he thought about this evening, the more he became so damn conflicted about his emotions.

There was a mix of emotions coming from all directions. Between this house and the letters he'd found from his grandfather, the prospect of selling the place, and everything going on with Violet, Brady wished like hell he had the answers. He wished he could see into the future to where he would ultimately end up and see if he was happy.

Violet was so fulfilled, so happy. She knew exactly what she wanted out of life and she was living each day obtaining her dreams.

For years, he'd wanted to build his career and one day make partner at a prestigious firm. He wanted his grandfather to be proud of the man he'd become, he wanted to prove to his father that he was important.

And here he was on the cusp of making that career goal a reality and his father didn't necessarily care and his grandfather was gone.

How could several weeks in one place trump all the years he'd been working? How could one woman, one town, one house have him reconsidering every thought he'd ever had?

Frustrated as hell, Brady called for Luna and they went back into the house. He put her food and water down and checked the time. The tour had been over nearly an hour.

Where could Violet be? He pulled his cell from his pocket and he hadn't missed any messages. He walked through the house with Luna right at his feet. He admired each room, wondering how soon Vi would start taking things down and staging it for the open house.

No doubt she'd whip right through that process as well and handle it all like the professional she was. But she was more than professional, she was proficient and fun and so full of life. She'd incorporated him into all of her world and she made him feel like he belonged there… but that couldn't be possible. Could it?

Brady cleaned up in the kitchen and tossed all of the empty boxes from Mad Batter. Another hour went by and still no Violet. He texted her and waited about ten minutes, growing worried when there was no response.

He didn't want to ask her mom or Robin or Simone. There was no need to worry anyone unnecessarily. Since it was getting late, he decided to take Luna in the old beat-up truck and drive around to look for Violet. She was a grown woman, but he hadn't heard a word from her since she'd been here with the tour, and it wasn't like her to just go off the grid.

Brady had Luna at his side and drove through town, going to Violet's shop first. Perhaps she had some work to get done there or maybe she went to her apartment, but her Jeep was nowhere in sight. He didn't see it parked near Robin's or Simone's places, either.

He didn't know where Lori lived, but he did know where Porter lived. When he drove by the mayor's house, still no Jeep.

And then he had a thought and turned toward the park. Thankful he'd put Luna in her harness and remembered her leash, Brady parked and hooked Luna up before heading down the path toward the gazebo. This was his last resort. Brady truly had no idea where she'd be if she wasn't here.

Sure enough, as he rounded the curve in the sidewalk, he spotted a flash of green. She stood with her back to him, her hands on the rail and leaning forward, staring up at the sky. Her headband was gone and that long, dark red hair curled down her back.

He paused on the sidewalk, wondering if he should just go and leave her be. Clearly she wanted time alone or she would've texted or come home.

Brady mentally groaned. He had to stop referring to his grandfather's house as his home or Vi's home. Neither of them lived there. It was a neutral ground for them to play house or have an affair...or whatever label this should be called. But it was not their house.

Just as he started to go, she turned and caught his eye.

"Sorry," he said, remaining still. "I just got worried when I didn't hear from you. I'll go."

He tugged on Luna's leash to get her to come with him, but Violet stopped him.

"You can stay," she called. "I'm sorry I didn't tell you I'd be late."

Brady shifted his focus back to her and still remained down on the sidewalk with Luna.

"You don't have to check in with me," he told her. "I only came out because I got worried after you didn't show up and then you didn't reply to my text."

"My phone is in the car." She crossed her arms and sighed. "The tour was a great success. Don't you think?"

He took a step forward, then another. "I do. Grandpa would be proud of all you did."

"It's not just me," she clarified. "There's a joint effort."

"Maybe so, but I know who the leader is and I know the driving force behind these community events." He stepped up into the gazebo, coming even closer to her. "So what's on your mind that had you coming here?"

She stared for a moment before turning back to look out at the night. Brady hadn't seen her like this before. The normally excited, bubbly woman had something weighing so heavy on her and he wanted nothing more than to fix it.

"Nothing but selfish thoughts," she murmured. "I just needed to recoup from the tour and cleanse my mind for a bit."

Brady took Luna out of the gazebo and tied her leash to one of the posts so she was down in the grass in case she had to do her business. Then he went back up and came to stand beside Violet.

"If I were a betting man, I'd bet that every year after the tour, you are still flying high and smiling from ear to ear."

She cast him a quick glance and shrugged before looking back into the darkness.

"I'd say that's accurate," she murmured. "Everything is different this year."

Brady swallowed a lump, not wanting to fully recognize the additional guilt. She was hurting and whether it be from William's passing or Brady coming into her life, he didn't know. All he knew at this point was he didn't want her to have regrets or remorse. When he left, he wanted to leave her with good memories. He wanted her to continue to have beautiful days in that Violet Calhoun world she lived in.

And he was starting to see he wanted to be part of that, but he didn't even think that was a possibility.

Chapter Twenty-Three

Christmas is only magical if you believe.
* Violet Calhoun

She felt ridiculous having a pity party. It was worse now that Brady was here. Violet had finished the tour, said goodbye to Lauren and Bryce, taken a few silly selfies with Robin and Simone, and ended up here. She hadn't gone back to her shop, her apartment, or Brady's house. There was a storm brewing within her, a storm she'd never experienced and she just needed to be alone.

Yet here he was and she didn't really know what to say. What was there to say? That she was finally coming to grips with the fact he was leaving in a month? That she had fallen in love with him, but she knew he couldn't say the same?

Anything she admitted now would only have him feeling guilty and destroying everything good between them. That was not how she wanted him to remember her.

Besides, they still had another month together and if she loved him like she claimed, then she would take what she could have. As much as she wanted to fight for him, she wouldn't make him choose between her and his career. That wasn't fair and that wasn't love.

Violet promised herself to remain strong, to be that rock he needed during this time, and when he was gone, then she could continue this pity party.

Turning to face him, Violet pasted on a smile. "This year was just different," she told him. "I miss doing all this with William. We'd always go back to his house and have cookies and milk and talk about how we pulled it off again."

Brady reached for her hand and squeezed it. "He'd be thrilled how this year turned out."

Violet nodded. "I know he would. He'd love that you were here for this. But I'm being selfish. I never asked how you were doing through all of this. I'm sure it's difficult being in his house without him there. I don't know why I never asked before now."

"It's fine." He reached for her other hand and stepped into her. "I'm doing okay. I was worried before I arrived and that first night was rough so I fell asleep on the couch."

Her smile quivered a little. "That explains the suit."

"It wasn't a suit," he defended with a grin. "Instead of spending all my time alone with my memories and my remorse, I was steamrolled by Santa's elf and I didn't have time to think of much else."

As much as she wanted to laugh over his description of her, there was something she wanted to know.

"Do you believe certain people come into your life for a reason?" she asked.

Continuing to hold her hands, he stared down into her eyes. "I never really thought about it before, but I'm damn grateful you were here for me during this time. Staying in that house all alone would've been depressing."

"You have Luna."

The dog in question let out a little bark and Violet peered over Brady's shoulder to see her roaming around in the grass.

"I wouldn't have Luna if I hadn't come here with you," he told her. "You've opened up my world to a whole host of things I never would've considered."

"You're keeping her, aren't you?"

He nodded. "I'd say we need each other. I couldn't give her away at this point."

No, they were a team. Violet released Brady's hands and wrapped her arms around his neck. She just wanted to feel him, to inhale that masculine scent, and seek comfort from his strength.

"Are you sure you're all right?" he asked, embracing her.

Violet nodded against his shoulder. "It's just a bittersweet moment, you know?" She eased back and looked into his eyes. "Sorry if I'm bringing you down."

"I asked because I want to know if something is wrong. Why do you think I came looking for you?"

The fact that he was worried warmed her heart.

"I assume that big-city mind of yours kicked into overdrive and you thought I'd been kidnapped or worse."

Brady narrowed his gaze. "Go ahead, laugh at me. I was only a little worried."

She pressed a quick kiss to his lips. "Well, I'm fine now. Ready to go?"

He stopped her before she could pull away. Something troubling stared back at her. She couldn't quite put her finger on it, but Brady seemed almost…worried.

"What is it?" she asked.

"Are you staying with me?"

The question hit her hard. Did he mean tonight or for the month? Or did he mean forever?

"Excuse me?"

"While I'm in town," he corrected. "Will you just stay with me? I know we haven't really talked about it and I know you've been there, but—"

"I'll stay."

He seemed to release a sigh like he'd been afraid to ask. She hadn't seen Brady afraid of anything. He seemed to tackle everything head-on and know exactly what he wanted.

Clearly, for now, he wanted her.

"Let's get Luna home," he told her.

"I drove, so I'll meet you back at home."

There went that word again. She was done fighting it. So what if she wanted to live in this fantasy world for another month? Some people went their entire lives never finding one minute of love. If she was only going to have it another few weeks, she was going to squeeze every ounce of love out of this short time.

Brady had been right. The whirlwind that was Violet came whipping through taking all the décor from the Tinsel Tour down. By Monday morning, she had everything put back into place, save for a couple of Christmas trees.

The telescope had been returned to the library and Violet had already brought in totes of décor and various items to help stage the home to get ready to sell.

Now, she stood in the living room talking to herself once again as she stared at the fireplace. She kept muttering *cozy* and *children reading*. He had no clue what was going through her mind and he felt it best to leave her alone.

"Are you going to need me?" he asked.

She glanced over her shoulder and blinked like she'd totally forgotten he was there. "Oh, no. I've got everything covered. Are you going somewhere?"

"Just to the study to straighten it up a bit. I think I have everything boxed that needs to go back with me and I have someone from the library coming to get the rest of the books that I decided not to keep."

"Wait," she said holding up her hands. "We need those spare books. Don't get rid of them just yet. I'll need them to fill the built-in shelves."

He nodded. "No problem. I'll call and let them know. It's not like I didn't already donate a ton anyway."

Brady went to the study and of course Luna was right at his feet. He'd just stepped inside when his cell vibrated in his pocket. He pulled it out and saw Mick's name on the screen.

"Hey, Mick."

"Brady, man, I'm sorry it's taken forever for your car," Mick started. "But it's done now. Would you like me to deliver it today?"

Brady laughed. "That would be great, but I'd gotten so busy, I didn't think to call and check on it."

"Well, I'm glad, but since I had it so long, I took a little discount off your bill."

"You didn't have to do that, but I appreciate it, Mick."

"Sure thing. And no rush on payment. If you want to put the keys out in the old truck, I'll bring your car in about an hour."

"Sounds good," Brady told him. "Thanks, man."

He disconnected the call and crossed to the old desk that had belonged to his grandfather. The old lamp and file divider still sat in the same spot that Brady had always remembered. He could still see William sitting there looking over the community events and trying to figure out what each age group would like. He always wanted everyone to feel involved. The man was one of a kind and Brady missed the hell out of him.

Brady's cell vibrated again in his hand and he glanced down expecting Mick again, but saw Frank. Wondering what he would need that couldn't be emailed, Brady answered.

A Monday morning call had to be important.

"Morning, Frank."

"Brady, is this a bad time?"

Brady glanced to where Luna had curled up on the large area rug in the middle of the floor. She'd adjusted pretty well to calling this house her home. He hoped she was just as flexible with a condo.

"This is fine," Brady replied. "What can I do for you?"

"I have some good news."

Brady walked over to the desk and took a seat at his grandfather's old leather chair. "And what's that?"

"I imagine you're ready to get out of Peach Grove," Frank began. "Corbin will be leaving sooner as it turns out. We're ready for you to come back."

Brady stilled. This was what he'd been wanting since first coming to town. He'd been waiting for the time to tick down and the moment when he could leave. But he didn't think that time was coming until the first of the year.

Suddenly, he wanted more time with this house, more time in town…more time with Violet. That's what his decision boiled down to. Violet.

How could someone who had just come into his life have so much meaning? Was it just because of their bond with William? Was it because they had such a strong intimate connection? Or was there more? *Could* there be more?

That was something he couldn't answer and he didn't know if he would ever fully understand his own feelings.

"How soon are you talking?"

"If you want to be here for the Friday morning meeting, that would be great. Corbin's clients have all agreed that they would like you to represent them."

Brady rubbed his forehead as so many unknowns rolled through his mind. To make this leap wasn't something he was expecting. Had Frank called a few weeks ago and made this offer, Brady would have jumped at the opportunity.

Now, everything had changed.

"Can I let you know?" Brady asked.

Silence filled the other end of the line for a minute.

"I figured you would accept this offer without hesitation," Frank replied. "Is something wrong?"

"No, nothing wrong. Just doing some final touches to the house before I can get it on the market." He pulled in a deep breath and rolled through his mind what all he'd need to do to be ready to head back to his regular life. "Friday morning will be fine."

"Great," Frank exclaimed. "We'll see you then."

Brady disconnected the call...a call that should've made him more excited than he'd ever been. This was the chance he'd been waiting on and he actually was excited, until he remembered he would be leaving Peach Grove and not coming back.

Once the house sold, there wouldn't be a reason for him to return. He and Violet had said this was temporary. She had her life and he had his. They were so totally opposite, but yet they were compatible in so many ways... maybe the most important ways.

He'd have to tell Violet about the call. He would let her continue working today since she was in her element. He didn't want to upset her. She'd been different since the tour and when he'd found her alone in the gazebo, and whatever was bothering her, she was keeping close to her chest.

Brady unpacked the books and put them back on the shelves. He took the boxes and folded them down, putting them in the recycle bin in the garage. He noticed Mick had already traded out vehicles so Brady went out to the drive to inspect the job.

After making an entire pass around his SUV, he couldn't see one thing wrong with it. He got in the vehicle and turned it around, backing it up to the garage so he could load the boxes he was taking back with him. He still had no clue where he could store these things in his condo, but he had an extra bedroom, so they'd have to go there for now.

Luna remained asleep on the rug, oblivious to anything going on. Since he was leaving in a few days, he'd better do some research on those doggy day cares. He hoped there was one near his office, but he also wanted one that had stellar reviews and would take care of Luna.

He took a seat back at the desk in the study and pulled out his cell to find a place. There were a few in downtown that looked promising. After about ten minutes of searching, Brady discovered that this was going to be one hell of a monthly expense.

Is this what single parents dealt with? Good grief. What did those people do who didn't have high income jobs? This was an issue.

Brady called two of the three places he'd found. He spoke to the owners and explained he had a puppy. He basically interviewed them because he wasn't giving his baby up to just anyone.

He'd gone soft over a little bundle of black fur. She'd now flopped onto her back, her front paws dangled by her chest and her back legs had fallen apart. He couldn't help but laugh at the way she slept without a care in the world.

He'd just hung up with Dogs for Days when Violet appeared in the doorway.

Just the sight of her had a substantial dose of guilt weighing heavy in his chest. She needed to know, but damn it, he didn't want to say anything.

And he honestly didn't know if he was afraid of hurting her or admitting that he'd hurt himself. Was he ready to go? That had been the plan all along, so how could he second-guess everything now?

"Wow," she said, glancing around as she came on into the room. "I'm impressed."

"I'm trying." Brady came to his feet and circled the desk. "How's the staging?"

She sighed and nodded. "Pretty good. I want to make it feel super cozy, especially since we're hosting the open house before Christmas. I want a family to see what they could have here next year. Hot cocoa and cookies by the fireplace while they put up the tree and sing Christmas carols. The home really is something out of a movie set and gives that image of a perfect, happy life."

He rested his hip against his desk. "Is there such a thing as a perfect, happy life?"

Violet moved to the leather sofa and sat on the edge, dropping her hands to her lap. "Well, I do think that's possible, but what would make my life perfect and happy wouldn't be someone else's perfect and happy."

He smiled. She always made sense and made life sound so simple when everyone else seemed to make things difficult. That summed up Violet, really. She saw and appreciated the simple things, she smiled and loved life no matter what. She'd made him a better person than he ever thought he could be.

"Why are you looking at me like that?" she asked.

Brady shook his head. "No reason," he said, coming to stand straight up. "So, what are you going to work on now?"

"I figured I'd take a break and grab some lunch. Care to join me?"

Their lives together had become so domesticated over the past few weeks. He couldn't say that he minded, but he also didn't know if this was the life for him. The only way to know for sure was to go back. He had to leave Peach Grove and find out which life was the life for him.

He couldn't lead her on anymore and he didn't want to play games. He'd never been that way and Violet definitely deserved the truth.

"I'm going back to Atlanta," he told her.

She stared at him for a moment before nodding. "I know."

"No, I mean in a few days," he amended. "One of the law firm partners just called and wants me there Friday morning."

Violet's eyes widened as she stared across the space. Then she pulled in a breath and stood. "Well, okay then. I guess we better get this house ready for the open house. Don't worry, you won't have to be here for that. I can host and hand out the information about the house."

She just kept talking, rattling things off in her mind, but he knew she was upset or irritated or nervous…likely all three.

"If you want to get a Realtor since you won't be here, you might want to look into that," she went on. "Unless you plan on coming back for any reason."

Brady closed the distance between them and reached for her. He rested his hands on her shoulders and stared down at her.

"Do you want me to come back?" he asked.

Violet tipped her head and offered a sweet, almost sad, smile. "Brady, we both knew you were leaving. I won't lie, though, I wanted more time with you."

That was an understatement. He wanted more time with her.

"Maybe prolonging this would only make it worse in the end," she added. "Leaving now is probably not a bad thing, even though we don't like it."

There she went again, making sense. She was absolutely right. The longer he remained, the harder it would be to leave.

"Do you have arrangements for Luna?" she asked.

"I was researching that just before you came in." He took a step back and glanced down to where Luna was waking up. "It's highway robbery what some of those places charge."

Violet laughed. "Well, you can always see how she does at your condo while you're gone. You've crate trained her."

"I know, but sometimes I'm gone ten hours and that's not fair."

Violet stared down at the pup and smiled. "I'm going to miss her."

"Does the same go for me?" he couldn't help but ask. "Are you going to miss me?"

Violet reached for him and looped her arms around his neck. "Do you even have to ask? I'll miss the hell out of you, but I'll never forget this time we had. I'm glad you let me put the house on the tour."

"You didn't leave me much choice," he joked. "But I'm glad, too."

Brady wrapped his arms around her and held her close. There was a burn in his throat and a sting in his eyes and he absolutely refused to admit he was getting emotional. This was what needed to be done for them to get back to their regular lives, but right now, it hurt like hell.

Chapter Twenty-Four

The heart that gives is always full.
* Violet Calhoun

Violet stared at the display of wineglasses and had the sudden urge to kick the stand beneath them and see them shatter. She just wanted to kick something or hit something.

Honestly, she didn't know what to do to get this bundle of nerves out of her system. Brady had told her yesterday he was leaving on Thursday morning. She only had two more days with him and today she was at the shop since Carly was out of town.

But she knew this day was coming. And as upset as she might be, she couldn't be sorry for the time they'd shared together.

She still didn't like this display, though. It wasn't her best work and she just wasn't feeling it right now. That had never happened before. Getting in new items was always like a little bit of Christmas. Opening each shipment and then redecorating her store was such a blast.

All she had the urge to do now was fill each of these glasses up and see how quickly she could numb that pain.

The front door chimed and her mother stepped inside.

"Good morning, sweetheart."

"Hey, Mom."

Her mom closed the door and started glancing around the area. She walked over to the new shipment of stockings and started sifting through.

"What are you out doing today? More wedding plans?" Violet asked.

"I just stopped by Robin's and finalized my flowers. I went with a simple white bouquet. I don't know what fancy name she had for the flowers, but they are going to be perfect with my pink dress."

Violet stared at the glass display. "That's nice, Mom."

"Honey, are you okay?"

Violet blinked and glanced up to see her mom had moved closer. Vi shook her head to clear her thoughts and forced a smile.

"Fine," she replied. "Just can't get this display right and it's frustrating. That's all."

"Well, maybe I can help."

Her mom picked up a couple of the clear stemless wineglasses with gold trim. She moved a few, then stepped back, and moved a few more.

"I don't think it was bad the way you had it," her mom finally said. "But I'm going to buy a few. Let me take out the ones I want and then you can start again."

She picked around and finally grabbed three. "These are so cute, Vi. I'll set them on the counter while I shop."

Violet stared at the hole her mother had made by taking out three glasses. Maybe she should do something different. Maybe she should make up a few gift sets with a bottle of sparkling cider just to show how they could be gifted with wine.

"Vi, what's going on?"

She turned her attention to her mother who still stood up at the counter. "Nothing. Why?"

"Because I said your name twice and you have been zoned out since I walked in."

Lori came around the counter and had that motherly look in her eye that said she wasn't buying the lie that Violet was telling.

"What is it?" she asked.

"Brady is leaving."

"He's always been leaving," her mom said.

"No. I mean he's leaving on Thursday," Violet corrected. "They called and wanted him back sooner so he's leaving before Christmas."

She'd shed a few tears over this in private, but she'd also had stern pep talks with herself that she had lived without him before and she would find her normal again once he was gone.

"Oh, darling, I'm so sorry."

Her mom started to reach for her, but Violet stepped back.

"I know you mean well, but please no hugs. I knew this was coming, but now that it's sooner, I'm just not ready."

"Did you ask him to stay?"

Violet shook her head and tried to focus on her display. She needed to stay busy and her store had always been her first love.

"I'm not asking," Violet said. "That's not fair to him. He has a life and a career in Atlanta, just like I do here. We never made each other any promises."

"I understand that, but things progressed…didn't they?"

"They did. That doesn't mean our circumstances have changed. Asking him to stay would be wrong. If he wants to stay, it has to be because he wants to and not because I asked."

Violet started putting all of the glasses back into the box so she could start over. Her mom helped her and they worked in silence for a few minutes. No doubt her mom was trying to come up with some grandmotherly advice that would save the day, but there was nothing that could be said that would change the outcome.

"Have you at least told him that you love him?"

Violet froze, her eyes darting to her mom. "I shouldn't be surprised that you know, but I am."

"You're my daughter, I know how you think. Besides, I saw how the two of you looked at each other during Thanksgiving. That's love and it's not one-sided."

Violet laughed. "Mom, he doesn't love me."

"Why? Because he hasn't told you? You haven't told him, either."

Violet's heart lurched to her throat and she swallowed all the emotions she didn't know how to deal with.

Did Brady love her? True, she had never told him, but she never guessed he loved her. He'd even said he wasn't sure about love or lasting marriages. He was a divorce attorney, for crying out loud. The man dealt with couples splitting up on the daily. No wonder he was so hesitant to believe some couples could make it work.

But if he wanted to see if things could work between them, that would be his call. Yes, she should go after what she wanted, but at the same time, she didn't want him to stay out of pity or if he wasn't sure they would work. All he would do was regret his decision later if so, and the last thing she wanted to be in his life was a regret.

"Mom, just let it go," Violet told her. "I've got two days left with him and I plan on enjoying them."

Her mom's brows drew in. "Then what are you doing here?"

"I own the shop," Violet snorted. "I can't just close. What note would I put on the door? Closed due to a bruised heart?"

Her mom rolled her eyes. "Where's Carly?"

"Out of town today. She'll be back tomorrow."

"Then get out of here and I'll take over," her mom ordered, waving her hands. "Go on. Get back to Brady."

"I can't just leave you to the store," Violet declared. "I have responsibilities."

"And one of those responsibilities is taking care of yourself," her mom countered. "Now go."

The few times Violet had been sick over the years, her mom had taken over so she was well aware of how to run things.

"You know you want to be with him," her mom added. "Your mind isn't here today."

"No, it isn't." Violet reached out for her mom and wrapped her arms around her. "Don't pay for a thing," Vi told her. "Take what you want and consider it payment."

Lori eased back and laughed. "I'll cover for you and still pay for what I take. Now, go to Brady and think about telling him how you feel."

As if she could think of little else.

Brady whistled for Luna to come back with the ball. "Drop it," he told her.

She stood at his feet with the ball in her mouth, wiggling her tail and staring up at him.

"You have to drop it so I can throw it," he laughed.

He went to pull the ball and she let out a little growl.

"Oh, you're a big ferocious beast."

Brady finally got the ball free and tossed it. Luna immediately went right after it.

"It's a beautiful day to be outside."

He jerked around to see Violet stepping out onto the patio. She'd pulled all of that mass of hair on top of her head and wore a long-sleeved T-shirt that read You Are the Holly to My Jolly tucked into her jeans. Her little red sneakers were adorable. Everything about her quirkiness was adorable.

"Shouldn't you be at the shop?"

She slowly closed the gap between them. "Mom is watching it for me. When she came in and I told her you were leaving Thursday, she insisted on covering for me."

Luna came back and ran to Violet.

"Hey, sweet girl. Give me the ball." Luna sat with the ball in her mouth. "No, you have to give it to me."

"We're still working on that. She always comes back, but isn't too quick to give up her ball."

"Come on, Luna." Violet's voice became a bit sterner. "Drop it."

The dog instantly dropped it and Violet flashed him a wide smile before she bent down to pick it up and throw it.

"Don't be jealous," Vi said, coming to stand next to him. "So, have you had lunch yet?"

"I've only had coffee today. You have something in mind?"

She slid her thumbs through her belt loops and nodded. "As a matter of fact I do. Just stay out here and I'll bring it out."

"You have lunch already?" he asked.

She was already walking away, but smiled over her shoulder before she disappeared back inside the house.

That woman was always keeping him on his toes. He honestly couldn't imagine life without her, but then he worried he was just caught up in the new, excited feelings of a relationship that always tingled like this at the beginning.

But had he ever felt like this? He didn't remember any woman making him feel the way Violet did.

Moments later, she came out of the house juggling a blanket folded over one arm, a large sack, and a drink carrier.

He quickly moved to assist her and took the bag and drinks. "What's all this?" he asked.

"I thought we could have a picnic," she told him, fanning out the blanket on the grass. "I wanted to go to the park, but since Luna is used to your yard, I figured we were safer here."

Details were seriously her default mode. She never left out anything or forgot anything.

"So what did you get us?" he asked.

"Well, I went by the café we love and grabbed those wraps." She pulled them from the bag and Luna immediately came over to sniff. "And I got sweet teas, plus they had their homemade kettle chips, so I have some of those, and the best part is…"

She pulled out a container and popped open the lid. "Red velvet cake. It is literally the best thing you'll ever have in your entire life."

"You were right on everything else I've tried there, so I'm sure it will be good."

"I also got something for Luna if you don't mind."

"What is it?"

Violet opened a foil packet and revealed a piece of grilled chicken. "I looked it up and grilled chicken is okay for dogs. I asked Suzette, the owner of the café, if she had any extra that I could buy for the dog."

Brady laughed. "Of course you did."

Violet tore up little pieces, tossing one at a time for Luna to go after. Each time Luna ran away, Violet would eat.

"What made you want to do a picnic?" he asked.

She shrugged and threw another piece of chicken. "I wanted to do something low-key and relaxing," she told him. "I also wanted it to be just us."

Us. That had a ring to it he couldn't deny he liked.

"Are you anxious to get back to your job?"

Of all the things he would've guessed she would say or ask, that sure as hell wasn't in the top ten. Brady assumed she was dodging the subject.

"I am," he answered honestly. "I miss helping my clients start a new chapter in life. I miss my colleagues."

"Are you comfortable with Luna in the city?"

Brady grabbed a kettle chip and thought. "All I can do is try. I've gotten so used to her, I can't remember my life without her."

Much like the woman in front of him, but he couldn't exactly say that. He couldn't find the words or bring himself to allow that type of exposure. He didn't know if this was real, not that he'd never felt *real* before.

But he knew she made his life better, he knew she made him smile with her eccentric ways, and he knew she had a heart unlike any he'd ever known.

"So you're going to be a partner?" she went on. "That's a big accomplishment."

He swelled a little with pride. "Thanks, but when I go back I'm still on a probation period."

"You'll get through it," she told him. "You're a deter-mined man and they're lucky to have you."

Luna came back after her last piece of chicken and started sniffing the bag, looking for more. She finally gave up and curled up on the blanket and settled in for a nap.

An uneasiness settled deep within him. Each day he grew more and more accustomed to this familial lifestyle… a life he didn't even know would attract him.

Going back to Atlanta was the answer. Settling back into the life he knew had to be the answer. He wasn't comfortable with change, and staying in Peach Grove was one hell of a change that he didn't think he was ready for.

Chapter Twenty-Five

It's a Christmas miracle when you say no
to a glass of wine.
* Violet Calhoun

Violet stood back and stared at the meal she'd made. She wasn't even sure it was worthy of the trashcan. How the hell had it all gotten so…dry? She'd followed the recipe. How could she fail at a recipe? It was literally just reading and following directions.

She'd wanted to surprise Brady on his last night here. She'd sent him out for a couple hours so she had time to prepare. Now he was going to come home to this. Not the surprise she had in mind.

The front door alarm chimed as Brady came in. Violet sighed and figured there was nothing she could change about this now. There wasn't much left in the fridge, either, since he was leaving and she would go back to her apartment.

"Something smells good," he told her.

She laughed as he stepped into the kitchen and glanced to the island where she had set what should have been dinner.

"Smells can be deceiving," she told him. "I attempted

lasagna because I knew you liked it. But, this doesn't look anything like what you made."

He came to stand next to her and stared down at the pan. "I'm sure it's fine."

Violet couldn't help but laugh again. "For a lawyer, you're a terrible liar."

He flashed her a grin before turning to the utensil drawer and grabbing a fork. Then he poked at the lasagna and attempted to cut a bite out.

"It does seem rather…rubbery." He continued to poke and then busted out laughing. "I can't even get a piece out. I'm afraid I'll pull the whole thing in one giant section."

She smacked his arm. "Oh, hush. At least we have bread. All I had to do with that was heat it up."

"Then we'll have bread and wine." He wrapped an arm around her waist and pulled her against his side. "Even though it didn't turn out, I'm glad you surprised me with something you knew I liked."

"I think maybe I should work on my culinary skills."

He turned her to face him, then framed her face. "We all have skills, Vi. Yours is throwing killer parties and events. Simone's is the kitchen. Robin's is gardening. You don't have to be perfect at everything."

Even though he made sense, she still wished her final surprise for him would've turned out.

Violet slid her arms around his neck and tipped her head up to him. "What wine do you want with your bread? I have a merlot or a prosecco."

Brady leaned down and covered her lips with his. She smiled into the kiss, loving how he went for a distraction. Her fingers threaded through his hair as she pulled him closer. She wanted all of him, as much as she could get, before tomorrow morning came.

Reaching for the hem of his T-shirt, she gave a yank and pulled back from the kiss just long enough to pull the shirt up and over his head. She tossed it to the floor as he went for the bottom of her sweater. Moments later, they were standing naked in his kitchen and reaching for each other.

Brady gripped her waist and lifted her to the island. She squealed as the cold hit her bare skin, but she slid her legs around his waist.

Brady was on her again, his mouth claiming hers as he filled his hands with every inch of her…at least that's what it felt like. His hands roamed, explored, touched in the most delicious way.

Arching into his touch, Violet shifted her hips until she was at the edge of the counter.

"Please," she whispered. "I need you."

Those three words held so much meaning, so much more than what was going on right now. He was fairly positive how Violet felt for him…and damn it, he couldn't deny his feelings were strong.

Brady eased into her and flattened his hands on her lower back, urging her forward. He jerked his hips in the same rhythm as her. She whispered in his ear, but he couldn't make out what she was saying. Those warm, sultry pants had an even stronger spiral of emotion pumping through him.

Would he ever be able to move on after her? Would he even want to?

Brady wanted to consume her, to hold this moment one last time. He slid his lips up along the column of her throat, over her jawline, and up to cover her mouth. She gave a gentle tug on his hair as her entire body jerked and stilled. Her knees tightened against his hip bones and Brady couldn't hold out any longer, either. He let himself go, he let her love consume him, because that's what this was. He was positive she loved him—she'd never said it and he didn't know if he wanted her to or not, but he knew she felt it.

After his body settled, Brady eased Violet off the counter and lifted her up into his arms. With one arm behind her knees and the other behind her back, he carried her from the kitchen and up the steps and toward his bedroom. Her head against his shoulder was the sweetest gesture. She fully trusted him. He'd never had anyone depend on him in any personal way before, but Violet had gone all in with him…just like she did everything else.

And he was leaving her with all of those feelings and nowhere to put them.

They had less than twenty-four hours and he sure as hell was going to make the most of it.

He was gone.

Violet hung up another wreath in her front window. She'd been selling these white fur wreaths like crazy and constantly restocking from the back.

Anything to take her mind off the fact that this was Friday morning and Brady was back in his office, back in Atlanta. He'd left yesterday morning and kissed Violet goodbye. The kiss *felt* like a goodbye. She was rather proud of herself that she'd held it together until his car was out of sight.

She'd cried, she'd eaten ice cream, she'd thrown a pity party in her apartment. She'd done all the cliché things women supposedly did with a heartbreak, but she didn't feel one bit better.

Violet had let Carly work yesterday, but told her she'd take Friday and Saturday. Now she wished she would've stayed home. She certainly wasn't in the mood for work. Well, not that she wasn't in the mood for it, but she felt like a zombie just going through the motions.

When her doorbell on the front chimed, Violet turned to greet a customer. Throughout the next several hours, it was busy enough to keep her occupied, but come closing time when she was balancing out her cash/credit receipts for the day, her mind started wandering again.

Did Brady have a good day? Did he feel right at home back in his firm and condo? How was Luna adjusting?

As she was adding in the numbers on her laptop, she got an email notification from Lauren.

Violet opened the message and was excited Lauren had sent her a mockup of the magazine article to see if she liked it or if she wanted anything minor changed, as they were ready to go to production.

Violet opened the attachment, scrolling through the article and pausing on the photographs. They were all absolutely stunning. The one with Violet, Simone, and Robin in the gazebo, the ones of them at their storefronts, and the tour photos were amazing.

But Violet stilled, her breath in her throat when she got to the one where she stood in the doorway of Brady's home with him sitting on the front porch. He leaned against the post, with one foot propped up on a step. That crooked smile hit her in the gut. This image seemed so…perfect. Everything about it screamed Christmas card material.

Unfortunately, that fantasy wasn't going to happen.

Moments after this was taken was when she realized her fantasy would never be a reality. If being in Peach Grove for the holidays didn't make Brady want to stay, nothing would.

She'd desperately wanted to tell him her true feelings. She wondered if she cheated him out of knowing by keeping everything to herself, but she'd been so damn torn. She didn't want him to have to choose, so she'd kept quiet, locking away her emotions deep into a pocket of her heart that only Brady owned.

Violet sent a quick reply to Lauren thanking her and Bryce for the amazing article and how fabulous it was. Vi couldn't wait to get copies of this magazine. She planned on framing the article and hanging it in her shop.

Once she closed her laptop, Violet set the alarm, turned off the lights, and headed up to her apartment. She could work some more on her mother's wedding arrangements, at least that would help occupy her mind.

That little burst of happiness that Vi held for her mother did help Violet's bruised heart. Her mother had found true love and they were finally joining as one. That's what Lori deserved. That's what Porter deserved, too.

Violet was excited to have him as part of the family and loved how he treated her mother like a queen.

Since her mom was getting married in the gazebo in the park, Violet wanted to have some massive pots with greenery and white flowers that would match the bouquet. Robin was working on ordering all the flowers needed. Violet borrowed some big pots from the garden club. She planned on stringing delicate strands of lights all across the inside ceiling of the gazebo to offer the romantic, elegant glow.

The dinner afterward was going to be at Porter's home. Violet had already set up a caterer and had round tables and chairs to set up out in his patio area. Even though it was an evening wedding, Porter had an enormous indoor and outdoor patio area, perfect for the reception.

Part of Violet wished she wasn't going alone. She'd so wanted Brady to be by her side. She wanted to share that special moment with him on Christmas Eve. She'd wanted to wake up Christmas morning in his arms.

Violet went to her bedroom to change and spotted the gift she'd bought for Brady. She could always mail it, but that seemed silly. They hadn't discussed talking beyond his departure, but she hoped he'd at least stay in touch. If he felt half of what she did, then his feelings were strong.

She didn't want to return the gift, either, so she decided to keep it. At least every time she used it, she'd remember him…not that she'd ever forget.

Her cell vibrated and it was a text from Brady. Her heart beat a little faster and she smiled like a teenage girl as she opened the message.

Missing you. Hope you had a good day at the shop.

Then a picture popped up and she couldn't help but laugh. It was a silly selfie with him and Luna again. He had on a navy suit—and here she'd just broken him in with wearing casual clothes—and Luna was licking his face.

Violet couldn't help the twinge of burning in her eyes and throat. Damn it. They'd only been gone since yesterday morning and it seemed like weeks had gone by.

She held her cell straight out, tipped her head and smiled, then sent him a pic.

Missing you guys! How was your first day back?

She waited while he typed and remembered the email from Lauren. He'd probably like to see those mockups as well. After all, he was a big part of the tour this year.

I had the best day. Probably the best one I've ever had here.

As much as those words hurt, that's also exactly what she wanted for him. She wanted him to live the life that made him happy. That's exactly what she was doing. That's what everyone should do. Small-town living wasn't for everyone and that was okay. She just wished it didn't hurt so bad.

I'm proud of you.

They said their goodbyes and Violet pulled up the email on her phone and sent it to Brady. Maybe when the magazine came out he'd like to get his own copy. Who knows, maybe he'd frame it so he could remember his time in Peach Grove?

Violet put on her pj's, grabbed a glass of wine, and settled in her bed to work on some more notes for her mother's big day.

All she could do at this point was move forward with her life and try to keep her heart whole because she feared it was on the verge of shattering.

Chapter Twenty-Six

*It's only a Merry Christmas with you
under the mistletoe.*
* Violet Calhoun

For the second day in a row, Violet was swamped at her store. The closer it got to Christmas, the more people panic shopped. Fine by her. That's what she lived for.

By the end of the day, she was exhausted. She hadn't heard from Brady since last night and she really didn't want to be the one to initiate a conversation. If he was trying to merge back into his old life, then he didn't need her confusing him.

She really wished she could take a nice, hot bubble bath, but her apartment only had a shower. That was just one way she'd gotten spoiled at the plantation. The huge garden tub in the master suite had been so luxurious.

A hot shower and cozy pj's in her old chair would just have to do. As she climbed the steps to her apartment, part of her wondered if she should get a little dog. She really missed Luna and any dog could be trained...she hoped. Maybe she could bring her pup to the shop on days she worked.

As she put her key in the door, she heard a bark.

Turning around, she glanced down into the alley and didn't see anything. She laughed, focusing back on her lock. Now she was hearing things because she was sleep deprived from a broken heart.

Her key turned easily, which was weird considering she always had to jiggle it just right to get in.

The moment she opened the door, she jumped at the silhouette of a man. She screamed before she realized.

"It's me," Brady said.

Luna ran forward and pawed at Violet's leg. She squatted down to pet the dog and tried to get her heart to beat normally again.

"What are you doing here?" she asked, glancing up to Brady. "And how did you get inside?"

He took another step forward, shoving his hands into the pockets of his jeans. "I went by Porter's house and asked your mom for a key."

Confused, Violet stood. "But why aren't you in Atlanta?"

"I don't want to be."

Violet blinked, then closed the door at her back, still trying to process everything. "What do you mean you don't want to be? Did you get fired?"

Brady laughed. "No, I didn't get fired. I turned in my resignation."

"Excuse me?"

He took a step and then another as he narrowed the gap between them. "I resigned from the firm."

Violet rubbed her forehead. "I don't understand. You texted me last night that you'd had the best day. What happened?"

"I did have the best day," he told her. "When I got there, I went into the meeting with the partners. They all could see that my heart wasn't in it and I just told them that I think I'd changed my mind. Maybe Atlanta isn't for me anymore."

Violet's heart swelled. She wanted to throw her arms around him, but she also wanted him to finish what he came all this way to say.

"I fell in love with Peach Grove," he went on. "I loved it as a kid, but I see everything so differently now. I see why Grandpa took part in everything with this town. And maybe selling the house is a bad idea."

"What?" Violet couldn't help the laugh that escaped her. "I'm having an open house next weekend."

Now he reached for her and Luna ran across the living room out of the way. Violet flattened her palms against his chest and stared up at him.

"Cancel it," he commanded. "Because that's where I plan on spending the rest of my life."

He rested his forehead against hers. "With you," he added.

Violet jerked back. "With me?"

Terrified he was making a mistake, she eased from his grip and started pacing. When pacing wasn't enough, she went to her bedroom to escape him and gather her thoughts.

But he followed and loomed in her doorway with some naughty, knowing grin on his face.

"You can't do that," she told him.

"What can't I do?" he asked. "Ask you to spend your life with me? You love me, Vi. I know you do and I love you. That's why I'm here. A day apart was too damn much."

She shook her head and held up her hands. "You don't mean that. As much as I want all of that to be true, I'm afraid you'll resent me and have regrets. What happens in six months when you decide you made a mistake?"

He stepped into her room until he stood directly in front of her. With his finger, he tipped her chin up so she had no choice but to look at him.

"Never going to happen," he told her. "I'm already making plans for my new life here. I'm going to talk with a few firms, I'm even entertaining the prosecuting attorney position. But I will be here…with you."

She closed her eyes and let all of his words sink in. Maybe he did know what he wanted, maybe Peach Grove was for him…maybe she was for him.

"Please be sure," she murmured. "I can't stand to see you leave again."

He kissed her forehead. "I only left to give my resignation in person." He kissed her nose. "And I had to be sure my love for you was real." He kissed her lips. "The moment I resigned, I knew I had to pack my things and come right back."

She opened her eyes and focused on him. "How did you know I love you?"

"Because I love you," he said simply. "I knew in my heart how you felt."

"I didn't want to confuse you."

"I'm not confused," he admitted. "Not anymore."

She pulled him closer and rested her head against his chest as she held on. She never in her life thought he'd be back.

"Is that a telescope in the corner?" he asked.

Violet pulled away and glanced over her shoulder. "I bought that for your Christmas present. I was hoping you'd decide to stay and I know you loved the one of your grandfather's, but since the library has it, I thought we could start our own tradition with this one."

Brady picked her up and spun her around. "I'm never letting you go," he told her. "I want my house here to be ours. After seeing that image you sent last night from the magazine, I knew I'd made the right decision. That picture just felt right."

Violet's eyes welled up and she couldn't stop the tears.

"I never understood happy tears," he joked. "At least, I hope those are happy tears."

"Very happy," she told him. "Does this mean you'll be my date to my mother's wedding?"

He lifted her, carefully laying her on the bed as he came to lie on top of her.

Resting his hands on either side of her face, Brady kissed her softly and said, "I'll be your date every day for the rest of your life."

* * * * *

Reviews are an invaluable tool when it comes to spreading the word about great reads.
Please consider leaving an honest review for this or any of Carina Press's other titles that you've read on your favorite retailer or review site.

To find out more about this author, visit her website: julesbennett.com.

Acknowledgments

First, I have to thank God for giving me a life, family, and career I absolutely love. I am one blessed woman!

Next, to my family. Michael, Grace, and Madelyn are absolutely my entire world.

Huge thanks to Elaine Spencer for always being right there holding my hand or giving me the push I need to step outside the box. I am forever grateful for our journey and can't wait to see where we are headed.

I cannot let a chance go by without giving a huge shout-out to Jessica Lemmon. I'm not sure I'd make it in this roller-coaster industry without her. From lake plotting to FaceTiming with wine, we've literally been through it all. Personal, professional… I know she's always there for me when I need anything at all.

For Jill, my amazing assistant who is also a great friend. I love that I send her a text to check into something and she's not only done it, she's already moving on to the next item I didn't even know I had on my to-do list. She is truly my right-hand woman.

And to my readers… THANK YOU! Without you, I wouldn't have my dream job of living in a fantasy world that takes me places I literally dream of. Whether you get my books from stores, online, from a friend, from your library...thank you for the support!

About the Author

USA TODAY bestselling author Jules Bennett has penned over eighty novels and novellas since she first published in 2005. She's married to her high school sweetheart and together they raise two girls in their home in the Midwest. Jules loves to travel and is always using her destinations as inspiration for the next book. She absolutely loves to chat with readers and can often be found on social media.

JulesBennett.com
Twitter.com/julesbennett
Instagram: jules_bennett
Facebook.com/authorjulesbennett

*Also available from Harlequin Desire
and Jules Bennett
in her Dynasties: Seven Sins series is*
Hidden Ambition.

*Will she be his ruin...
or his redemption?*

*Revenge has never been hotter—
until desire burns away their deceptions...*

Chase Hargrove is on a mission to take down the company
that destroyed his family...by becoming its CEO. Loyal
Black Crescent employee Haley Shaw is his unwitting secret weapon. But when Chase is blindsided by passion for
her, he gets careless. With his hidden motives exposed,
will he lose everything—even Haley? Or will the tables
turn when he learns she has hidden motives of her own...?

*Read on for a preview from
Hidden Ambition by USA TODAY
bestselling author Jules Bennett.*

Chapter One

Haley Shaw bent over the gift boxes, searching around the obscene bouquets of flowers and cupcake boxes, just trying to find her damn yellow highlighter.

"That's quite a display."

The low, throaty voice was all too familiar...and all too arousing.

Haley straightened and turned to face a smirking, sexy Chase Hargrove. The persistent man was vying for the coveted position of CEO of Black Crescent Hedge Fund. The successful investment firm had been through hell and back, and Haley had stuck through it all—which made her the target of all the résumés and all of the bribes. Hence the gifts cluttering her normally pristine work space.

"I assume you were referring to the flowers and boxes and not the fact I was bent over with my backside facing you while looking for my highlighter," she stated, smoothing down her conservative dove-gray pencil dress.

His deep brown eyes held hers. "Of course."

Sure. That naughty grin gave him away and she had a feeling a powerful man like Chase always held his emotions and cards close to his chest. He wanted her unnerved, thrown off track. Well, it would take a hell of a lot more than charm and a little flirting to really get her attention.

Haley prided herself on her professionalism. She'd worked too hard, overcome too much, to land where she was. True, she was an executive assistant, but she had power here at Black Crescent and she never let her emotions, or a man, get in the way of her duties.

Not even this sexy man who was very qualified to take over the coveted CEO position and potentially become her boss.

"Do you have an appointment?" she asked, knowing full well he didn't.

Chase had been popping in and out over the past several weeks, ever since Josh Lowell had announced he was stepping down and the CEO position would be available. Chase had turned in a rather impressive résumé and had even landed an interview a few weeks ago. The position had been offered to Ryan Hathaway, but ultimately, Ryan turned down the coveted title. So the search continued as Chase moved closer to the top of the list. Hence Chase pursuing the job…and her.

Not that she minded a sexy distraction, but she really did need to get her work done and there was no chance of that as long as Chase stood at her desk with that panty-dropping stare.

Maybe he really was here for the job, but he spent an exorbitant amount of time charming her.

Haley was Josh's right-hand woman and everyone thought she was the gatekeeper in regards to the top position. Haley had to admit, she didn't hate all of this attention. Who could be mad when cupcakes, flowers and chocolates were delivered on the daily?

"I do have an appointment," he amended with a naughty, crooked grin. "With you."

Confused, she crossed her arms over her chest. "Me?"

"For lunch."

Oh, he was a smooth one. He thought he could waltz in here, pour on the charisma and she'd just take him up on a day date? Clearly he knew nothing about women… or at least this woman. She didn't let anything interrupt her work. Or at least, she never did before him.

"I'm not free for lunch." She lifted one vase, then another, on her desk, glancing for all the things she'd lost in this chaos. "But you go have a nice time."

"What are you looking for?" he asked, obviously in no hurry to go.

"My highlighter," she informed him. "I keep getting all of these gifts and I've run out of room for things I actually need. I normally have everything in a designated spot, but now…"

She tossed her hands up, frustrated with how quickly her space had become unorganized.

"When we go to lunch, we can stop and get you as many new highlighters as you need," he suggested. "My treat."

Haley glanced up and really wished her belly would stop doing those schoolgirl flops over a hot guy and his offer to buy her dollar markers.

So what if his shoulders perfectly filled out that black suit jacket? So what if his messy hair looked like he'd just rolled out of his lover's bed? He wouldn't be rolling out of her bed, so she really had no place fantasizing about such things.

She had important issues to tend to and getting distracted by a man who likely wasn't interested in her, but in how far she could get him in this field, was not one of them.

The phone on her desk rang and she sighed. "If you'll excuse me, I need to get back to work."

She took the call and moments later when she hung up, she was surprised to see he had actually left. But there wasn't a doubt in her mind that Chase Hargrove would be back. A man like that never gave up.

Chase clutched the surprise in his hand and headed into Black Crescent Hedge Fund for the second time that morning. Determination and revenge were a combination that no rejection could penetrate.

No matter how many times he had to show his face, flirt a little or buy silly bribes, he'd sure as hell do it. A little humility was nothing in comparison with what his family had gone through at the hands of Vernon Lowell.

The sneaky bastard had squandered millions and disappeared fifteen years ago, but Chase would never forget the struggle his family went through after his father was framed by Vernon to take some of the fall.

Chase's father had landed in prison for a few years, paying for his actions after Vernon had left a neat and tidy paper trail leading right to their door.

Now Chase had the opportunity to seek his own justice, since Vernon was never caught. His son Josh was now at the helm, and Chase didn't find him exempt from the damage.

He hadn't counted on the perks of the revenge plot, though. Getting an eyeful of Haley Shaw was certainly an added bonus. There was something about her unruffled attitude that made him want to just get his digs in where he could…which was why he didn't mind one bit that she'd caught him staring at her ass.

He wasn't a jerk or a guy who took advantage of women. He respected women, but if a male held the position that Haley did, Chase would certainly be going about this via a much different route.

As he stepped through the double glass doors, he nodded to the receptionist and headed toward the elevators. One day soon, this would all be his. Chase had the credentials and was more than qualified to settle perfectly into the CEO position. But if not, then he'd at least get the scoop he needed to help bring Black Crescent down for good. They deserved nothing less and Haley was inadvertently going to help him.

As for the top slot here, Chase didn't need it. He sure as hell wasn't hurting for money, but he wouldn't mind adding another investment firm to his portfolio.

Chase stepped out of the elevator and walked toward Haley's large circular desk, and once again the overwhelming scent of flowers assaulted him. He shouldn't be surprised at all the candidates vying for her attention, though they were being too predictable. Boxes of gourmet chocolates? Oversize floral arrangements? Cupcakes from the local bakery? Please. Those candidates were amateurs and utterly boring.

Haley had her back to him and was holding a stack of papers, muttering beneath her breath. A woman getting caught up in her work was damn sexy, but he wasn't here for seduction. Shame that. Having Haley under different circumstances wasn't something he'd turn down. Classy, smart, powerful… She was the entire package of sex appeal.

Chase pushed lustful thoughts from his head and

tapped his knuckles on the edge of the desk. She startled and glanced over her shoulder, her wavy blond hair framing her face.

"Back so soon?" she asked, quirking a brow.

Damn if her sarcasm didn't up his attraction to her. He had to admit, this challenge wasn't proving to be boring. He actually looked forward to his interactions with Haley.

Chase held up the present. "I brought you something."

Her eyes darted to his hand and she turned fully to face him. "Seriously?" She laughed as she circled her desk. "Is that a bouquet of highlighters?"

He extended the gift. "You couldn't find yours and you had enough flowers and gourmet-cupcake boxes."

She stared at the bundle for a second before she took the variety of colors. The wide smile on her face was like a punch of lust to his gut. Not exactly what he'd come looking for, but something about her simple style and natural beauty appealed to a side he didn't want to be appealed to.

Lust and desire didn't follow guidelines, though. He couldn't help this attraction and he couldn't help but wonder if she was getting that kick of arousal, as well.

"Well done," she told him with a wide grin. "I admire someone who thinks outside the box."

Chase shoved his hands in his pockets. "Admire enough to go to lunch? You do get a lunch break, right?"

"I do," she confirmed. "But I'm not going to lunch with you. I have other plans."

"Cancel them."

She cocked her head. "Are you always demanding?"

"When I see something I want."

And there it was. A glimpse of desire he hadn't quite been sure about flashed through her eyes. Well, well,

well. Maybe he could keep working this angle and come out with the job and a side fling. Win-win.

"Fine," she conceded. "We'll go to lunch, but we will not talk business."

Not talk business? No problem. He could gather information from her without her even realizing he was doing so. He hadn't gotten this far making billions by not being able to read people.

Besides, he'd already worn her down—by a bouquet of highlighters, no less. Chase was confident he would get damaging intel from her and she wouldn't have a clue she'd even let him in.

"Lead the way," he said, gesturing to her door.

Chase followed those swaying hips and reminded himself he was here for a purpose, a vendetta, not to see how quickly he could slide that zipper down and have her out of that body-hugging dress.

Only time would tell which one of them came out on top… But Chase didn't intend to lose.

Don't miss
Hidden Ambition *by Jules Bennett,*
available wherever Harlequin ebooks are sold.

www.Harlequin.com